Go

God made you for a purpose

A book about the power of hope, the gift of friendship, the meaning of life and the wisdom to find purpose in suffering.

By John Baptist James

Finnomir

On a big blue ball circling the sun.
On a continent unknown and unsung.
In a forest that has no name.
There grows a tree in the middle of a clearing.
And amidst the twigs and leaves and acorns,
Finnomir the butterfly was born.

*

From all corners of the forest good and decent animals travelled to the clearing to witness the great spectacle that was about to happen on that spring day early in the morning. Mr. and Mrs. Fox and their baby were the first to arrive on the meadow, and they sat down in front of the large tree. The herd of wild boar were next to arrive. Grunting and snorting, they trampled through the grass and sat down with the foxes. A young boar had just made itself comfortable when the ground suddenly vibrated under its rear. It jumped up startled, looked down and saw a molehill rising slowly. The mole stuck his head out of the mound of earth. He looked left and right, then blinked at the boar.

»Am I late?«

The wild boar grunted angrily and replied:

»No. It has not started yet.«

The mole smiled delightedly and nodded. He put his sunglasses on, crawled out of the ground, picked a straw of grass, laid back comfortably on his mound, yawned long and loudly and then nibbled on the straw.

Then the hares hopped up and sat down in the meadow. The deer made themselves comfortable at the edge of the forest. The mice and the birds had come, and the ram had travelled down from the mountains for two days.

»I watch that every spring«, he said to one of the stags when suddenly a loud roar and rumble sounded from afar, and all the animals looked startled towards the tree line where they saw Mrs. Bear storming onto the meadow. When she saw the animals staring at her, she stopped immediately. She blushed and grinned sheepishly and scratched herself behind the ear.

»Excuse me. Was I too loud? I was worried I wouldn't make it in time.«

Embarrassed, she tiptoed across the meadow to accompany the

other animals and she greeted them all warmly. She looked around and found a good spot to sit in and dropped onto her massive bottom. The ground shook and the mole fell off his mound.

»Hey! Can't you be more careful?«

Mrs. Bear blushed and scratched her ear again and then she sat there silently, waiting for the big event to start.

*

After a while the meadow was filling up with more animals and it became noisy in the clearing. The youngsters hopped around and played, and the adults were chattering away, when suddenly a shadow passed across the sky and all the animals fell silent immediately. They looked up and there was the eagle. He circled in front of the sun and descended in a spiral until he finally landed on the meadow. The animals looked at him in awe and bowed to him. The eagle looked back at them and bowed too.

»Greetings to all of you, good animals of the forest.«

Then he looked up at the tree.

»I see I have come at the right time, because its already

starting.«

The squirrels quickly climbed up the tree trunk, spread out over the large branches and looked excitedly at the treetop. Crackling noises were coming from above, and one of the squirrels pointed a finger at a low hanging branch and called out loud:

»Here comes the first one!«

A cocoon was hanging from the underside of a large green leaf. The lower end of the cocoon expanded, just like a bubble before it bursts. Then it tore open right in the middle and the head of a butterfly appeared through the crack. The butterfly wriggled back and forth, squeezing out of the cocoon little by little until finally its rump slipped out of the tube that had been its home for so many weeks. The newborn member of this world sat on the green leaf and blinked, and it saw the world for the first time with its butterfly eyes. Another squirrel jumped up and down on a branch nearby excitedly.

»Here comes the next one!«

Then everything went fast. One butterfly after another slipped out of its cocoon. First there were two of them, then ten, then a hundred, until finally thousands of newborn butterflies filled the treetop. The mole had jumped up from his mound, climbed up Mrs. Bears arm and stood on her shoulders. He pointed towards the treetop and cheered:

»Look! They are unfolding their wings.«

All of the animals held their breath in excitement. The wings of a thousand butterflies grew bigger and bigger, and the green treetop turned into an ocean of purple and blue moving spots. The animals of the forest cheered »Ahh« and »Ohh« in joy. This was the moment they had been waiting for; it was the sight they had been looking forward to see since the end of winter. The butterflies began to flutter their wings and the treetop rustled louder and louder.

»They'll be flying straight away«, said the eagle. He spread his mighty wings and fanned them.

»Fly, my friends, fly! I know you can do it. Just flap your wings hard!«

And a cloud of purple and blue fluttering wings rose from the treetop and slowly descended to the grass. The butterflies landed on the blooming flowers of the meadow and they drank their first nectar. Now they were strengthened and rose up in the air again and they hovered over the gathered animals' heads for a moment and chorused:

»Goodbye! Goodbye!«

They rose higher towards the sky and flew across the meadow and over the forest and out into the world. The animals of the forest watched them leave until the purple and blue cloud of butterfly wings blurred into the blue of the sky and they disappeared beyond the horizon.

*

A long and peaceful moment of silence covered the clearing. Then one young wild boar sniffed:

»That was nice.«

Now everybody sighed. The mole had fallen around Mrs. Bear's neck. He clenched her and howled and cried tears of joy. Then he wiped his nose in her brown fur, climbed down her arm quickly and disappeared headfirst into the hole in the ground. The eagle looked up at the tree and nodded in satisfaction, while the baby fox nudged his mother with his nose and asked:

»What are the *flutterbees* doing now, mom?«

Before mother fox could answer him, the eagle leaned down to him and said:

»They are called *butterflies*, my little friend. And now

they fly out into the world and pollinate the flowers, like the bees and the bumblebees. Then they look for a spouse and make babies. They lay their eggs and after a while the eggs become caterpillars. The caterpillars spend the winter in dry leaves and in the spring they build a cocoon on this tree and a new generation will be born again, just like today.«

The baby fox listened carefully to the eagle and replied:

»Then I have to come back next spring. As I would like to see this again.«

The eagle laughed.

»Quite a little fox. I will be here as well.«

*

By and by the animals left the clearing. The deer were the first to disappear into the forest. The birds had flown back to their nests. The wild boars rummaged through the soil with their noses for a while before they left. Only the eagle, the ram and Mrs. Bear remained. They stood silently in front of the tree and watched the squirrels scurry around the branches inspecting the empty cocoons. Then the ram spoke:

»Well, my friends. I have to leave you now. It is a long

way back to the mountains.«

»I'll accompany you«, said Mrs. Bear, and the two said goodbye to the eagle. They were just about to leave when turmoil broke out in the treetop and the eagle called up to the squirrels:

»Hey! What's going on up there?«

One of the squirrels replied:

»There's another one. He won't come out.«

The eagle, Mrs. Bear and the ram stepped closer to the tree and the squirrel showed them a small cocoon, only half the size of the others. It hung under a leaf and fidgeted wildly as the butterfly inside struggled to get out. Again and again he kept pressing his head against the bottom of the cocoon, it bulged but it did not split open.

»Shall I help him?«, asked the squirrel. »I could nibble on the cocoon a bit.«

»No!«, the eagle shouted sternly. »He has to make it on his own.«

The squirrel patted the cocoon and spoke to the butterfly inside.

»Hello, little one, make an effort! Press a bit harder

just a few more times and you will get out.«

When the squirrel had said that, the cocoon stopped fidgeting for a moment and a faint voice could be heard from inside.

»Open up, you stupid door!«

With a forceful thrust the cocoon suddenly tore open, the butterfly stuck out his head and he was breathing hard with relief.

»At last! I was worried I would never get out of here.«

Then he squeezed his body out of the tube and sat on top of the green leaf to take a rest. The squirrel called down to the eagle:

»He made it. He is out.«

Then the squirrel disappeared into the treetop. The eagle, Mrs. Bear and the ram watched the little butterfly for a while and waited to see how he unfolds his wings, but it did not happen.

»Hello butterfly!«, said the eagle. »You have to pump up your wings to unfold them!«

The butterfly turned around and saw the three large animals standing far below in the meadow.

»But I have pumped them up already.«

The eagle looked at his two companions with concern, then he spoke to the butterfly again.

»What's your name, little butterfly?«

»I'm *Finnomir*. And who are you?«

»I am *Aquila*, the eagle. I am Lord of the skies. This is *Mora*, the she-bear from the deep forest. And this is *Pito*, the ram from the high mountains.«

Finnomir crawled over a branch and from there climbed down the tree trunk to get closer to the three big animals. There he sat down and looked at the animals below.

»I think something is wrong with my wings. When I flutter I still cannot fly.«

Now the eagle and his companions could see. The butterfly's wings were far too small and shriveled. Mrs. Bear stood on her hind legs and held out her hand to Finnomir.

»Climb into my hand, Finnomir! I'll help you down.«

»Mora, wait!«, said Pito the ram. He looked at the eagle and whispered.

»What use is it if we help him, Aquila? He won't be able to fly anyway.«

The eagle contemplated for a moment, then he turned to Mrs. Bear.

»Help him down, Mora, and put him in the meadow! That's all that we can do for him.«

Finnomir climbed into Mora's hand and she carefully placed him in the grass. He just stood there for a moment and looked at the three animals.

»I heard what you said. I will never be able to fly, will I?«

He sobbed and looked down on the ground sadly.

»What shall I do now, Mr. Aquila?«

The eagle leaned down to him.

»Look at me, Finnomir!«

Finnomir raised his head and looked into the eagle's eyes. And the eagle spoke:

»You will have to wander the earth on foot, Finnomir. You walk through the grass, climb flowers and drink nectar. And at night you will lie down to sleep under a large leaf.«

Then they were all silent for a moment.

»Well, that doesn't sound too bad«, said the ram suddenly. »Now that that's settled, I can go back to the mountains. Are you coming with me, Mora?«

Mora looked at the ram, worried.

»No, Pito. I will stay with Finnomir a little longer.«

The ram shrugged his shoulders.

»Fine. As you like.«

Then he left and made his way back to the mountains.

»I'll leave you now too«, said the eagle. »Goodbye, Finnomir. I wish you all the best.«

Then he looked at Mrs. Bear.

»Don't stay in the clearing too long, Mora!«

The eagle turned around, flapped his wings and rose into the air, and Finnomir watched the majestic bird flying high up into the sky until he disappeared behind a cloud.

»I want to fly like an eagle too«, he said.

Then he sadly lowered his head and sat down.

»But I probably never will.«

Mora contemplated for a moment, then sat down next to Finnomir.

»I can't fly either, Finnomir. I also have to walk around the world on foot and you will see that is not a bad thing.«

Finnomir looked at her pensively.

»Do you really think so?«

Mora smiled.

»Of course.«

Then she pointed at a flower.

»You should have something to eat. Why don't you climb up this flower and drink the nectar?«

Finnomir got up on his feet and did what Mora advised him to do. He went to the flower, climbed up the stem and sat on the blossom.

»You see? It works wonderfully«, said Mora.

Then Finnomir stuck his head deep inside the calyx and drank five mouthfuls of the sweet nectar. When he pulled his head out the nectar stuck to his lips. He wiped his mouth clean, looked at Mora and smiled.

»Mmm! That tastes good.«

Then he looked across the meadow.

»There are a lot of flowers here. I will probably have enough to eat, even if I cannot fly to other meadows.«

Mora smiled.

»I like your attitude, Finnomir. That's the spirit. You will see that you will want for nothing here.«

Then Mora got up.

»I have to go back to the forest now. I wish you all the best, Finnomir.«

Mora left and Finnomir watched her disappear behind the trees of the forest. There Mora started to cry, but Finnomir did not hear that. Finnomir was now alone. He sat on the flower and made plans about what to do next, and there he remained until the evening.

*

Finnomir was watching the sunset when a voice came from the ground.

»Hey, you there! Up there on the flower.«

Finnomir crawled to the edge of the flower petal and looked down. A grasshopper stood on two legs and looked up. He had his other four arms on his hips. Finnomir looked at him in amazement.

»Yes, how may I help?«

The grasshopper jumped up from the ground and landed on a large green leaf right next to Finnomir's flower.

»You're new here, aren't you?«

»Yes. I hatched today.«

»Well, well,« said the grasshopper and examined the little animal. Then he scratched his head.

»And what exactly are you?«

Finnomir bowed, coyly.

»I am a butterfly. And my name is Finnomir.«

The grasshopper frowned.

»A Butterfly? But what's wrong with your wings, Finnomir?«

Finnomir looked sad and sniffed.

»I do not know. It seems they didn't grow properly. They are too small and I am unable to fly.«

The grasshopper rubbed his chin.

»Aha, I see.«

Then he put his arms back on his hips.

»Well, my new meadow dweller. I am *Krix*, the fastest grasshopper in the clearing. I collect and spread the newest of all new news and I'm telling you, you can't stay up there on the flower. It will be dark soon and you should find a place to stay overnight.«

Finnomir looked across the meadow.

»And where should I go?«

The grasshopper jumped up from the leaf, did a somersault and landed elegantly on the meadow floor.

»Come with me, Finnomir! I know a place that you will like.«

Then he hopped off while Finnomir climbed down from the flower. He called after the grasshopper:

»Please wait! I cannot catch up with you when you jump so quickly.«

Krix stopped and looked back at Finnomir.

»Oh, forgive me. What was I thinking? We can just walk there on foot. It is not far from here.«

Then Finnomir and Krix wandered through the meadow until they reached the edge of the forest. When they arrived it was already dark and Krix held out his four hands.

»Tadaaa!«

He pointed to a cluster of large mushrooms under a tree.

»Here you will have a roof over your head, Finnomir. There is soft moss under the mushrooms and you can cover yourself with a fallen leaf.«

Finnomir went to the largest of the mushrooms and tested the moss underneath by stepping from one foot to the other a few times, then he smiled at the grasshopper.

»Thanks, Krix. It's very cozy here.«

Krix bowed.

»Always at your service, Finnomir. And now I bid you good night.«

Krix hopped away and Finnomir watched him disappear in the high grass. Then he collected a large leaf that had fallen from a tree. He lay down on the moss under the mushroom and covered himself with the leaf. Before he fell asleep, he thought about his first day in this world.

»I have a place to sleep and a whole meadow filled with flowers filled with nectar to drink. Maybe everything will be fine after all.«

Then he pulled the leaf over his head, turned on his side and fell asleep. That night he dreamt of flying up to the clouds together with the eagle.

*

It was the next morning. The birds started chirping and the first rays of sunlight tickled Finnomir's face and he woke up. He yawned, stretched his arms and legs, pushed the leaf aside and stood up. Some water droplets had formed on the edge under the roof of the mushroom. He stretched up and washed his face with the morning dew. Refreshed and fully awake he laid out the leaf properly under the mushroom, for this was now his house, and he decided that he would sleep here every night from now on. He went straight into the meadow and climbed up the first flower that had opened its blossoms and drank nectar for breakfast. Then he climbed the highest thistle he could find and looked across the clearing in every direction. He closed his eyes and took a deep breath. When he opened his eyes again, he smiled.

»Today I am going to explore the clearing. And over there, where the sun is just rising, that's where I will go first.«

He climbed down from the thistle and started walking. He wandered through the meadow and struggled through the jungle of grass, but after a while the grass grew thicker and soon he could no longer squeeze through it so he climbed up a flower and saw that he had almost reached the other side of the clearing. Since the grass had grown so dense, he just kept walking on top of it. He hopped from one blade of grass to the next, sometimes climbing over large, broad leaves, sometimes over long, thin leaves. Then he saw a colorful flower and it smelt wonderfully sweet. He was very hungry from wandering through the clearing for many hours, so he climbed up the flower to drink some nectar.

»Don't move!«, a voice called from behind. Finnomir turned around. He wanted to see who was talking to him. But suddenly the leaves of the flower started to fold up around him. The flower was closing and Finnomir was caught inside.

»Jump out!«, the voice yelled again, and Finnomir climbed out of the flower as fast as he could. He could just pull his legs out before the plant had closed completely.

»Get down here!«, the voice said sternly. Finnomir climbed down and there was a mouse standing in the thick grass.

»Good afternoon«, said Finnomir.

The mouse brushed its mustache.

»This afternoon almost ended in a very bad way for

23

you, my friend. You climbed into a carnivorous plant.«

Finnomir looked at the flower that smelled so sweet, and only now did he realize the danger he had been in.

»Thanks for the warning. My name is Finnomir and who are you?«

The mouse looked at Finnomir curiously.

»I am *Eric*, the field mouse. What are you doing here anyway?«

Finnomir shrugged.

»I hatched yesterday and now I'm exploring the clearing. I got hungry and wanted to drink nectar.«

The mouse rubbed a finger on his nose and twirled his whiskers.

»Fine, fine. But these flowers are dangerous. Memorize the color and the smell well. You may drink from all of the other flowers.«

Finnomir nodded.

»Thank you for saving me. I will remember this flower for sure.«

The mouse turned and started to leave, but then stopped,

looked back and scratched his head with a thoughtful expression on his face.

»Finnomir? I am currently taking a tour of the clearing. I could show you some nice places. Would you like to come with me?«

Finnomir grinned.

»Oh yes. That would be great.«

But then his face grew sad.

»But I can't fly after you. There's something wrong with my wings.«

The mouse nodded.

»I know you can't fly. Krix has already spread the news about you all over the meadow.«

Then Eric waved at Finnomir to join him.

»Just climb on my back! I will carry you.«

Finnomir smiled again. He climbed on Eric's back and held on to his fur. The mouse started to run and for a couple of hours they crossed the clearing in every direction. Eric showed Finnomir the walkable trails that led through the thick grass. He showed him the wasp nest that he should watch out for. He showed him a few holes in the ground to hide in, except when it was raining. He showed him where the most beautiful flowers grew and he introduced Finnomir to almost all of the inhabitants of the clearing. Eric patted a mound of earth and the mole came out and they chatted for a while. Then they met the frog on the way to his pond and they visited the new family of birds that had built their nest in a tree at the other end of the clearing. Finnomir was out with the mouse all day and then the sun started to set.

»It's getting late, Eric. I should go back to my mushroom house at the edge of the forest. But we walked back and forth so much that I no longer know the right direction.«

Eric smiled and twirled his whiskers.

»No problem, my little friend. The clearing is circular and the forest is all around it. All you have to do is walk along the edge of the forest no matter in which direction and you will always arrive at the same place. And should you ever get lost, just come to the big tree. It grows right in the middle of the clearing and can be seen from everywhere. Animals go there all the time and you can ask them for help.«

Finnomir thanked Eric for a wonderful day and they said goodbye. Then Finnomir did what Eric had told him to do. He walked along the edge of the forest and it was not long before he arrived at his mushroom house. There he climbed on a flower and had a large gulp of nectar for dinner. He stayed on the flower for a while and, like the day before, he watched the sunset. When the sun finally disappeared behind the mountains and twinkling stars appeared in the night sky, Finnomir lay down in his mushroom house, covered himself with the leaf and slept soundly.

*

Many happy weeks had passed and summer had arrived. All that time, Finnomir spent every day the same way. He woke up at sunrise, drank nectar, walked through the clearing and chatted with the other animals. He listened to Krix, the grasshopper, who told him the newest of all the newest news and in the evening he went back to sleep in his mushroom house.

One day, Finnomir was wandering through the clearing when he saw something fluttering in the air. He climbed up a blade of grass and watched this strange thing. When it came closer, he recognized it. It was a butterfly just like him. The other butterfly sat on a flower a short distance away and drank nectar. Excited and happy to finally see

27

someone like him, Finnomir waved and called:

»Hello, you there!«

The other butterfly was a girl and when she finished drinking nectar she looked at Finnomir.

»Yes? How may I help you?«

Finnomir ran to her across the leaves as fast as he could. When he reached her, he sat on a flower in front of her and smiled.

»Hi there. I am Finnomir. And what is your name?«

The butterfly-lady looked at Finnomir suspiciously.

»My name is *Karal*«, she said with a proud tone.

Finnomir was beaming.

»Karal. What a beautiful name. Would you like to stay with me for a while? We could become friends.«

Finnomir blushed when he said this. He ducked his head between his shoulders as if to crouch.

»And...and maybe...maybe we could start a family together?«

Karal eyed Finnomir from top to bottom and she grimaced as if she had eaten something unappetizing.

»You don't even have real wings.«

She shook her head contemptuously.

»I'm not wasting time with you. Have you ever seen what you look like?«

The butterfly lady spread her wings and fluttered away and Finnomir watched her leave. Then he sat there until evening came when Krix hopped by. The grasshopper saw Finnomir and realized that something was not right.

»Finnomir? Is everything okay?«

Krix hopped up on the leaf and sat next to Finnomir. He saw Finnomir's sad face and noticed that his friend had been crying.

»Don't you want to tell me what happened?«

Finnomir sobbed.

»No. I don't want to.«

He wiped his nose dry, then climbed down from the flower and went straight home. Krix called after him with concern, but Finnomir ignored him. At home, he lay down to sleep in his mushroom house and he dreamed again of having splendid wings and of flying up high above the clouds.

*

In his dream Finnomir flew with the eagle, but suddenly he noticed his wings were too small and he started falling. He fell towards earth faster and faster, and just before he hit the ground, he woke up from his dream, startled. It was still night time and the full moon was shining bright in the starry sky. It was quiet, only a few crickets chirped. Finnomir could no longer sleep, so he got up and went out into the meadow. He walked aimlessly through the trails of the clearing when he heard the frog croaking in the distance and so he went to the pond. The frog lay motionless in the water, only his eyes and mouth were visible above the waterline. When the frog saw Finnomir approaching he inflated his sound bubble and croaked:

»QUAK, Finnomir? What are you doing here? It's not morning yet.«

Finnomir did not answer. He stood at the edge of the pool and stared into the water and at this moment he saw his reflection in the bright moonlight for the first time, and he was terrified. His wings were terribly malformed. He turned his shoulders to the side to get a better look. They were not even half the size of normal butterfly wings, they were shriveled and had almost no color. A terrible pain grew in Finnomir's chest and a tear

30

ran down his face. The tear fell from his cheek and landed in the pond and Finnomir's reflection disappeared in the ripples. Finnomir had seen enough. He turned and left. The frog stuck his head out of the water.

»QUAK! Where are you going, Finnomir?«

Finnomir stopped, but did not look back to the frog. He looked up at the starry sky and contemplated for a moment. Then he sobbed.

»I will go into the dark forest.«

He wiped the tears away and wiped his nose clean, then he left the pond and went back to his mushroom house. When he got there, the sun was beginning to rise. He climbed up a long blade of grass and looked across the clearing one last time.

»Fare well, my dear friends«, he said softly.

He sighed, then descended from the blade of grass and looked in the direction of his mushroom house. The forest began beyond, and there was only darkness between the tree trunks. Finnomir started walking. He went past his mushroom house and straight into the forest. In the shadow of the large trees the world was dark and the air was cold. There was no grass growing and there were no flowers blooming, and the ground was covered with brown, dead pine needles. Finnomir just kept

31

walking and he would not stop until something ended, either the world or his life.

Rogo

Finnomir had been walking deep into the forest all day long with slumped shoulders and his eyes looking down sadly at the ground before his feet. He never looked up and he never looked back. Suddenly there was a rustling in a thicket nearby. Finnomir stopped and looked. He saw the leaves of the shrubbery shaking and a growling sound rang out from behind. Just one heartbeat later a large grey beast jumped out of the bush and stood up in front of Finnomir. He looked up and saw jagged teeth, long fangs and dark evil eyes gazing down on him. It was a wolf. He growled:

»What... are you doing... in my forest?«

Steaming, stinking breath came with the voice and Finnomir turned his face away to avoid the smell. Then he stared at the big animal for a moment, wondering what would happen next. First, he was scared, but then he simply smiled and bowed his head politely and walked past the wolf as if he did not care. The wolf watched Finnomir walk away and growled again in anger. He could not believe that this little creature was just ignoring him. He hissed furiously, jumped over Finnomir to block his way and shouted at him:

»I asked you: What are you doing in my forest?«

Finnomir stopped and looked up into the wolf's dark eyes.

»Is this really your forest?«

The wolf's eyes grew even bigger and glistened and he breathed heavily as if his anger would now turn into pure wrath upon Finnomir's daring question.

»Yes, it's my forest«, he yelled. »And whoever enters without my permission will be eaten.«

Finnomir thought for a moment, then shrugged.

»All right. If you want to eat me, go ahead.«

Then he smiled at the wolf, nodded kindly and continued walking. The wolf was speechless. His lips began to quiver as if being hateful had been too exhausting. He licked the dripping saliva from his sharp teeth, shut his mouth and swallowed hard. His hind legs started to tremble as if all strength would leave them any moment and his rear sank down and he fell on his buttocks. Sitting there the wolf looked at this strange intruder who dared to wander through his forest. The wolf was confused and shook his head in amazement. He scratched himself behind one ear with his hind leg and pondered for a while until he had an idea and a smirk formed on his face. He jumped up and ran after the little butterfly until he caught up with him and then he strolled jauntily alongside Finnomir. The wolf grinned sheepishly and spoke:

»I could pull out your little legs, you know? What do you think about that?«

Without stopping, Finnomir looked at the wolf walking by his side.

»I doubt you can grab my little legs with your big paws.«

The wolf stopped, held up a paw and looked at its front and back. Baffled, he stared up at the treetops and scratched his ear once more. Then he grinned again and continued walking alongside Finnomir.

»But I could easily crush you with my paw.«

Finnomir stopped and looked up at the wolf.

»Say wolf. Why are you just talking about it and not simply doing it?«

The wolf stared down at Finnomir dumbfounded.

»Aren't you afraid of me at all?«

Finnomir shook his head.

35

»No. I don't care if you eat me or crush me or pull my legs out. If you want to do it, just do it.«

They stared at each other in silence for a moment, then Finnomir continued walking. The wolf was stumped. He let Finnomir move on, but he followed him at a distance to spy on him. He wanted to know more about this little creature that was not afraid of him, because all animals were afraid of him and nobody dared to go into his forest. This little butterfly had made him curious.

*

Night came and Finnomir became tired. He looked around to find a place for the night and maybe something to eat for dinner. He had left the clearing without any breakfast or lunch and his hunger grew by the minute. In this dark forest there were no flowers to drink nectar from, only trees with brown bark, dead brown pine needles on the ground and a thicket here and there.

»No dinner tonight«, Finnomir sighed.

Under an oak tree he found a dry leaf and took it. He leaned back on a big root and covered himself to protect from the cold of the coming night. When he looked up, he saw the stars twinkling through the gaps between the tree tops and it reminded him of the night sky above the clearing. This was his first night away from home and the thought made him homesick. Although he had left the clearing just this morning, it felt like a different time. Nothing more than a memory of a different life in a different world.

Finnomir's thoughts were interrupted by the noise of twigs breaking underfoot. The wolf appeared between the trees in the distance. He had been following Finnomir the entire time and Finnomir knew that. He could hear his footsteps all the time and when the wind blew in his direction he could smell the wolf's awful breath. The big grey animal laid down next to a shrub not far away from Finnomir's lair. For a moment, they looked at each other and Finnomir wondered what the wolf might be up to, but he was too tired, too hungry and too homesick to worry about anything, so he turned to the side, pulled the leaf over his head and fell asleep quickly.

*

The next morning came. Something tickled Finnomir's face and he woke up. With his eyes still closed he recognized the foul smell that was blowing around his nose. When he opened his eyes, he saw the wolf leaning over him and sniffing him.

37

Finnomir grimaced.

»Yuck! You should wash your mouth! You have quite bad breath.«

The wolf pulled his snout back and squinted his eyes but he did not say anything. He just turned, took a few steps back and lay down at the place where he had spent the night. He rested his chin on his legs, looked at Finnomir and watched him curiously. Finnomir pushed the leaf aside, stood up and yawned. He looked around and then turned to his strange companion.

»Are you there, Wolf!?«

The wolf raised his head in surprise and blinked. Finnomir looked at him and rubbed his stomach.

»Are there any flowers with nectar in this forest? I'm really hungry.«

The wolf grimaced and put his chin back on his paws.

»Why would I care about your hunger?«

Finnomir scratched his head and pondered. He walked over to his companion and as he approached, the wolf raised his head quickly and sat up straight, alarmed as if the little butterfly unsettled him. He stared down at Finnomir suspiciously.

»What do you want!?«

Finnomir smiled and shrugged.

»You could do me a favor and eat me right now. It is faster than starving to death.«

The wolf eyed Finnomir for a moment, then he lay down again and rested his head on his paws like before. He turned his face away and said:

»I don't think I would like how you taste.«

Finnomir walked a few steps to the side so he could look the wolf in the eye again.

»But you haven't even tasted me yet. You can spit me out if you don't like my taste. The important thing is that I will be dead.«

Annoyed, the wolf turned his head away from Finnomir once more.

»Leave me alone!«

Then he got up, shook his fur, turned around and walked away. Finnomir called after him:

»Where are you going, Wolf?«

The wolf stopped and looked back over his shoulder at

Finnomir.

»You are not afraid of me. That isn't fun.«

Then the wolf trotted away and disappeared in the shadow of the forest.

*

The wolf was gone. It was still early in the morning and Finnomir set off again. Maybe he would find another animal that would eat him and he hoped it would not take too long because the feeling of hunger in his stomach was horrible. He carried on and after a while he saw a few rays of light shining through the treetops. The light shone on a small patch of forest floor, where some grass was growing there. He ran towards it and saw flowers.

»I hope there is something to eat there.«

He reached the little oasis, climbed onto a flower and looked into its calyx. It had nectar! He drank and the feeling of hunger disappeared quickly. Relieved, he sat on a large leaf and looked up through the openings between the treetops. Bright blue sky covered the world above this dark forest. He thought of the clearing and his friends.

»Do Krix and Eric miss me?«

The thought made Finnomir very sad, and the sadness made him tired. He lay down on that leaf and let the sun's rays shine on him. Then he fell asleep.

*

Finnomir woke up and the world moved around him. He saw the treetops slowly swaying overhead. The world was shaking up and down and something moved under his body. He tried to get up, but he could not. He turned his head and looked and he saw a company of ants marching in a long trail. They had tied him up and a worker carried him on her back.

»Hey! Excuse me! Let me down, please!«, Finnomir called, but the ant did not answer. He wriggled back and forth trying to free himself from the shackles, but he failed.

»Hold still up there!«, the ant scolded.

»What's the meaning of this? Where are you taking me?«, Finnomir asked.

»Into the burrow, of course«, the ant replied. »You're food for our younglings. Now stop fidgeting!«

Suddenly the world turned dark. They had entered the ant

41

burrow and they carried Finnomir through narrow and dim corridors. He got scared and started screaming:

»Help! Please let me go! Help! I want to get out of here. Help!«

The ants ignored his shouting and carried him to a dark cave. They put him on a stack of green leaves, and there they left him alone. Finnomir kept shouting for help, but after a while the strength of his voice left him and his courage had left as well. Robbed of any hope he gave in and wept softly in the darkness. Suddenly the whole anthill shook and the ceiling of the chamber started to crumble. The roof of the chamber broke up and a grey paw reached through the opening. A squad of soldier ants crawled over the intruder's paw and sprayed it with acid but it did not retreat. The paw reached for Finnomir and pulled him out of the burrow, and Finnomir saw daylight again. It was the wolf. He had freed him. He held Finnomir in his paw and with one claw he opened Finnomir's bonds and lifted him up on his shoulder.

»Quickly! Climb into my fur!«

So Finnomir did.

»Hold on tight!«, said the wolf, then he started running.

The wolf raced through the forest, leaped over roots and fallen tree logs, and scurried nimbly through the thickets. Finnomir held on to the wolf's grey hair all the time. Then the wolf jumped over one last bush and landed at the edge of a pond. There, the sun was shining bright, lush grass was growing and colorful flowers were in full bloom. The wolf went to the pool and dipped his paw in the water to mend the stinging pain of the ants' acid attacks.

»Ah! Oh! That feels good.«

He shook the water off his paw, then spoke to Finnomir:

»You can come out now. We are safe.«

Finnomir climbed out of the fur and the wolf put him down in the grass. They both sat on the edge of the pond, the wolf licked his paw, and Finnomir watched him.

»Why did you rescue me?«

The wolf stopped licking his wounds and looked at Finnomir.

»Why did you scream for help when you want to die? This morning you still wanted me to eat you. What made you change your mind?«

Finnomir looked down at his reflection in the water and pondered for a while.

»I don't want to die. What I really want is to have big, gorgeous wings and I want to be able to fly like any other butterfly, but that doesn't work with my wings. So what meaning does my life have anyway?«

Only now did the wolf recognize Finnomir's small, malformed wings.

»Oh! I understand.«

Then he scratched his head.

»Hmm!? Maybe there is someone who can help you.«

Finnomir's eyes widened.

»For real?«

»Yes. *Regula*, the turtle. She lives right over there on the other side of this pond. She is very old and wise. You could ask her for advice.«

Finnomir looked across the pond but couldn't recognize anything on the other side of it.

»Could you take me there? Please!«

The wolf held out his paw and smiled.

»Of course I can take you there. Get in my hand, I'll put you on my shoulder.«

44

Finnomir climbed into the paw and the wolf lifted him up.

»By the way, my name is Finnomir.«

»And my name is Rogo.«

Finnomir smiled at the wolf.

»Glad to meet you, Rogo.«

The turtle

Rogo and Finnomir walked around the pond and it did not take long until Rogo suddenly stopped at a place where the ground was covered with moss and where tall reeds grew all over from the tree line to the shore. A fallen tree stretched from the edge of the forest to the waterside. The bark was rotten and by the looks of it all of its branches must have broken off a long time ago. Rogo pointed towards the log.

»Do you see the fallen tree over there? That's where the turtle lives.«

They went to the tree trunk and Rogo knocked on it.

»Regula? Are you at home?«

A few moments later, they heard scraping sounds and a moaning voice coming from underneath the ground and two gigantic eyes behind thick glasses gazed at them from a hole under the log. It was Regula the turtle. She stuck her head out of the hole and her neck grew longer inch by inch. She squinted her eyes a few times, making the frames of her glasses wiggle up and down on the tip of her nose.

»Is that you, Rogo? What do you want? Can't you find

another innocent animal to annoy?«

Rogo lifted Finnomir off his shoulder and put him in front of the turtle.

»I'm not here to annoy you, Regula. I want to introduce you to someone. This is Finnomir. He is a butterfly and he needs your help.«

Finnomir smiled at the turtle.

»Good afternoon, Madam.«

The turtle looked surprised.

»Madam? No one has called me that in a long time.«

She inspected the little butterfly from top to bottom and sniffed at him, and her big eyes blinked under her glasses.

»I see what your problem is. It's the wings, isn't it?«

»Yes. They were so small from the day I was born, making it impossible for me to fly.«

The turtle twitched her nostrils a few times, and the glasses wiggled up and down like before.

»Well, come on into my cave. Let's see what I can do for you.«

Finnomir looked back at Rogo nervously, but the wolf nodded

in agreement.

»It'll be fine. Just go. I'll be waiting out here.«

And so Finnomir followed the turtle into a tunnel deep underground until they reached a large chamber with walls of moist clay and with stones and tree roots protruding here and there. In the middle lay a boulder that served as a table. A crystal vessel was standing on top of it with a flickering light shining inside. Finnomir climbed up on the boulder and looked at the wondrous light curiously.

»What's this?«

The turtle turned around and squinted her eyes.

»What's what?«

She saw Finnomir staring at the pulsating light.

»Oh that?! That is a lamp. My friends the fireflies made it for me. So I can read my books here underground.«

The turtle pointed to a wall with shelves filled with plenty of books.

»This is my library. Maybe we can find a solution to your problem in one of these books.«

She went to the shelves, raised herself on her short hind legs and pulled herself up on the first board. She stretched her neck, and her head moved slowly back and forth from left to right, scanning the shelves from top to bottom.

»I think I've read about a case like yours before.«

Her head stopped moving and she stared at a thin book. She pulled it out, read the title and shook her head.

»No, that's not it.«

She put the book back and looked at another one.

»Hmm. Maybe this one?«

She looked at it briefly and put it back immediately.

»No, not the right one either. Where did I put it? Ah! There it is.«

She grabbed a large tome from a shelf below. It was heavy and she had trouble pulling it from the board. She tucked it under her arm, lowered her body off the shelf and moaned:

»Oh! I'm getting too old for such climbing exercises.«

With the tome under her arm, she approached the table. She placed the book in front of the flickering firefly lamp and opened it. First, she browsed through the pages quickly, skimming the text casually, but then she stopped on a page that had a drawing on it. She tapped her finger on it.

»Right here! I knew it. There is the description.«

She stuck her head forward and brought her eyes so close to the book page that her nose almost touched the paper. Then she started reading aloud:

»Small, malformed wings from birth. The condition is called butterfly disease. Butterflies born with this disease cannot fly. Currently no healing method is known.«

Finnomir crawled up on the book and looked at the page. There was the drawing of a butterfly who, like himself, had wings that were small and shriveled. He looked at the turtle and shook his head questioningly.

»No cure?«

Then he lowered his head sadly and started to sob. The turtle twitched her nostrils a few times, causing her glasses to wiggle up and down like before.

»Not so hasty, young friend. There may be someone, a specialist in rare cases. Perhaps he can help you.«

Finnomir stopped sobbing immediately. He wiped his nose clean and a big smile formed on his face.

»Really? Where can I find him?«

The turtle rubbed her tired eyes under the glasses and yawned.

»Well, that's the problem. The specialist is a medical crab. He lives by the sea.«

Finnomir climbed down from the book and looked at Regula a bit puzzled.

»What is the sea?«

The turtle closed the book, tucked it under her arm, and walked back to the shelf. She looked up at the board where she had pulled the book out just a minute before but paused and groaned.

»Never mind«, she said and simply put the tome on the bottom shelf.

»The sea, you ask? Well, the sea is a large amount of water. It's an ocean that is infinitely larger than the pond in front of my doorstep. Some people say the sea has no boundaries at all.«

Finnomir scratched his head. He tried to imagine such vastness, but did so in vain.

»And there is this medicine...Uh...medicinecraaa ..«

»...Medical crab«, said the turtle. »Yes, he lives by the sea. But that's very far away. In order to get there, you would have to hike over the mountains and on the other side you would have to travel a large distance through an unknown world with unknown perils. Even if you could fly, the journey would take many weeks. But on foot? I do not think that is possible.«

Finnomir thought about Regula's words for a moment, then his shoulders sagged in disappointment.

»Thanks for your help, Regula.«

He crawled off the table and walked slowly through the tunnel back to the exit of the cave. The turtle followed him. When Finnomir came out of the cave Rogo recognized the butterfly's sad face.

»And? What did she say?«

With slumped shoulders Finnomir went to the edge of the pond and stared at his reflection in the water. Then he looked across the pond toward the mountains in the distance with their peaks reaching far up into the blue sky.

»There might be help, but I can't reach it.«

Rogo went and sat down next to Finnomir.

»Can you tell me more?«

Finnomir pointed towards the mountains.

53

»I would have to climb over the mountains and then travel to the ocean. A medical crab lives there, he's a specialist in rare cases and might be able to help me, but Regula says it's too far away. I can't get there.«

Rogo listened to his little friend and they sat there quietly for a few moments. And while Finnomir only experienced sadness in this silence, Rogo felt something quite different going on inside of him. He looked at the mountains far away and suddenly he had an idea that made his heart start racing. He jumped up, wagged his tail and shouted excitedly:

»Finnomir!«

Finnomir was confused and startled over Rogo's behavior.

»What's going on, Rogo?«

The wolf had a big smile on his face.

»What if I take you there, Finnomir? What if I get you over the mountains and from there to the ocean?«

Finnomir blinked in surprise.

»What do you mean?«

»Well. I could carry you. You should know that I can run as fast as the wind blows.«

Finnomir looked at the mountains, then looked at Rogo and

started smiling.

»Would you really do that for me, Rogo?«

Rogo nodded excitedly and his smile grew even bigger. Then a voice appeared from behind.

»Wait, Rogo! Not so fast!«

Regula had been standing behind them all the time and she had been listening to their conversation. She shook her head.

»Don't make promises to the butterfly that you can't keep!«

She pointed towards the mountains.

»You know what's waiting for you up on these mountains, Rogo. Don't you?«

The smile on Rogo's face disappeared immediately. He looked at the mountains thoughtfully, then he looked at the ground with a worried expression and pondered for a few moments until he took a deep breath and looked at the turtle with his head raised confidently.

»Don't you worry about that, Regula. I will take Finnomir to the ocean, no matter what. If everything goes well and his wings are healed he will be able to fly back home.«

The turtle shook her head and sighed.

»Oh, Rogo! Even if you could make it to the ocean, it would already be autumn here, and Finnomir would come back in winter. Where should he find food then? And you have to keep in mind that there is no guarantee that the crab can help the little one.«

Rogo began to get angry. He stamped his paws furiously on the ground, he shook his head, grimaced, growled and yelled:

»But we have to at least try! Just sitting around doing nothing doesn't make anything better.«

A smirk grew slowly on the turtle's face until her grin reached both ears. She blinked her eyes under her thick glasses and nodded contently.

»Rogo! I didn't know you could be so positive!«

She laughed and slowly turned around and crawled back towards the cave. The turtle was satisfied; she had achieved what she had set out to achieve. Without looking back at them, she said:

»It will get dark soon. You should stay here for the night and leave tomorrow early in the morning. I wish you both good luck.«

Rogo and Finnomir watched the turtle disappear in the hole under the tree trunk, then they looked at each other and smiled. They sat on the bank of the pond and watched the sun go down behind the mountains. Tomorrow morning they would start their journey.

When the sky finally became dark and the stars came out, Finnomir went to sleep. That night he dreamt that the medical crab healed his wings. He dreamt of how he would fly home and greet his friends in the clearing from the sky above. They would be amazed by his flying. It was a wonderful dream.

Rogo stayed awake a little while longer. He looked at the mountains with concern, remembering Regula's words. *You know what's waiting for you up on these mountains.* Yes. He knew what the turtle meant and he sighed.

»I hope it goes well!«

Then he too went to bed. But Rogo's sleep was restless that night.

The mountains

The next morning Rogo woke up at first light. He stretched his back and yawned loudly. When he shook his fur and looked around, he saw that Finnomir was already up and moving. The little butterfly climbed up a flower that had opened its blossoms and he stuck his head into the calyx to drink the sweet nectar. With every sip the butterfly took, Rogo could hear sounds of *»Mmm!«* coming from the inside of the flower. Finnomir pulled his head out of the calyx and the sweet remnants of his breakfast were around his mouth. Rogo laughed:

»Does it taste good?«

Finnomir wiped his face clean and licked the nectar from his fingers and he grinned.

»It never tasted better.«

»Good«, said Rogo and held out his paw and Finnomir climbed down from the flower and up Rogo's arm and he sat down on the wolf's fury shoulder. Rogo looked at the little butterfly.

»Are you ready?«

»No one has ever been more ready than I am now.«

»Very well. Then let us set off to the ocean.«

The wolf started running. First, he trotted along the edge of the pond but when they entered the forest he ran faster and Finnomir had to grab on to Rogo's fur in order to not fall off. The wolf scurried through the thickets and ran slalom through the trees. Every now and then Rogo jumped over a fallen tree trunk and Finnomir liked that very much, because for a short moment it felt like he was flying.

*

For half a day the wolf roared through the wilderness with the little butterfly on his shoulder until they arrived at a small stream at the foot of the mountains and Rogo stopped there. His long pink tongue hung out of his mouth. He was out of breath and panting. He stared up at the steep, stony walls and swallowed hard, then he spoke to Finnomir:

»This is where the mountains begin. We must climb up there, but we should take a break first. I am hungry and thirsty.«

Finnomir agreed and Rogo took him off his shoulder and placed him on a small green patch of fern.

»Excuse me for a moment«, Rogo said and turned around and went to the edge of the little river. First, he drank a few sips to ease his thirst, but then he just stood there motionless and stared into the water for a while. Suddenly he jumped up and stamped his front legs right into the middle of the stream, the water splashed up, Rogo grabbed something with his mouth and then his snout wriggled back and forth wildly. He stepped out of the water and came back with a fish in his mouth. He sat down next to the butterfly and ate the fish and Finnomir watched the wolf and grinned.

»Now I know why you have such a bad breath.«

Rogo looked surprised for a moment but then realized that Finnomir was right. He started laughing loudly and with the laugh came a loud burp.

»Oh! I'm sorry. Where are my manners?«, he said but he let out one more belch. He blushed and covered his mouth with his paw and Finnomir burst out laughing too. When they had calmed down, Rogo finished eating his fish and Finnomir drank nectar from a flower nearby. They both sat there for a while and rested in the early afternoon sun, then Rogo held out his paw to the butterfly.

»Come, Finnomir! We should move on.«

Finnomir climbed up Rogo's arm and sat on his shoulder and Rogo trotted along the bank of the little river to the place where the steep cliff began. He pointed uphill.

»The water of this stream gushes out of a little crack in the rocks high up on this mountain. I know the place well. I have been there before. We follow the water uphill and at its spring we will spend the night.«

»How high up is that, Rogo?«

»Very high,« he replied, and he sighed, but then he looked at the butterfly on his shoulder and smiled.

»But it is an easy task for me.«

Just one moment later Rogo jumped on the first boulder that lay before him. From there he jumped to the next bolder, and to the next, step by step they moved up the steep and stony path. The higher they got, the less trees there were and dense bushes stretched across the ground making it more difficult for Rogo to find a walkable trail. When evening came, they finally arrived at the spring of the stream. From a small crack under a rock, the water trickled out gently and made its way down to the valley.

»We are here, Finnomir.«

Rogo bowed down and drank from the spring to allay his thirst, then he collected a patch of green soft moss for Finnomir to sleep on. He lifted the butterfly off his shoulder and placed him on his bed. Finnomir stepped back and forth on the moss to test its softness and smiled.

»Thank you, Rogo. It's a very cozy bed.«

»You're welcome!«, Rogo replied. Then he took a look around and sniffed the ground until he finally found a place that looked acceptable to sleep on. He turned around his axis twice then lay down and curled up his body, almost like a snake. He yawned and closed his eyes.

»Rogo?«

»Yes, Finnomir«, the Wolf replied, keeping his eyes closed.

»Do you actually know the way to the ocean?«

Rogo opened his eyes and looked at the butterfly.

»No. But I know the way over these mountains. A little further uphill is a plateau, from there we will get to a pass and on the other side we will find a little stream running downhill. We will follow this stream and it will lead us to the ocean.«

Then he yawned and rested his head on his paws.

»I am pretty exhausted, Finnomir, and we have a long journey ahead of us tomorrow. So If you don't mind, I'm going to sleep now.«

He took a deep breath and fell asleep immediately.

»Good night«, said Finnomir, amazed that someone could fall asleep so quickly. He looked around. There were no fallen tree-leaves, but he found the leaf of a fern that could serve as a blanket. He lay down on his bed of moss, covered himself with the leaf and fell asleep. They both slept soundly all night long.

*

When Finnomir woke up the next morning, the world was shrouded in fog.

»Rogo, wake up!«

First, the Wolf's ears wriggled, then he opened his eyes.

»What is it?«

»I can't see anything at all,« said Finnomir with concern.

Rogo stood up, stretched his back and yawned.

»It doesn't matter. I know these mountains so well I could walk around these parts blindfolded.«

64

Rogo put Finnomir back on his shoulder and they continued their journey. The wolf moved slowly and carefully so as not to make a misstep in the fog and as the morning grew older a light wind started to blow and gradually blew the fog away until the sight was clear. Rogo began to run faster and after a while they finally reached the plateau. Suddenly a voice sounded from above.

»Well, well, now look at that! Who do we have here?«

Rogo stopped, startled. He and Finnomir stared in the direction of the voice. A large wolf jumped from the rock above them, landed right in front of Rogo, and blocked the way for the two hikers. The strange wolf was much taller than Rogo. Finnomir was scared and crawled into Rogo's fur. The big wolf howled once, then five more wolves jumped out of every direction and circled Rogo. The wolves growled; they bared their teeth and one of them grinned maliciously.

»Boy oh boy. You have nerve to show your face here again.«

Another of the wolves sniffed in Rogo's direction contemptuously.

»So, you still eat fish?«

The other wolves burst out laughing.

»Fish...ha ha...«, and »Yes, yes, fish,« they giggled maliciously. The big wolf growled loudly and the other wolves were silent immediately. The big wolf bared his teeth.

»Why are you here, Rogo? Tell me why I shouldn't tear you to pieces.«

His voice was menacing, and full of hate. Rogo stood completely still in front of the big wolf. He raised his head proudly and showed no fear.

»I don't want anything from you, *Eratogast*. And I don't want anything from your pack either. I just want to cross the pass, hike down the other side of the mountains and from there travel to the ocean.«

Eratogast stared at Rogo in disbelief. Growling, with his head lowered, ready to attack, he circled Rogo slowly.

»To the ocean? What do you want there? Aren't the fish in the streams of the forest big enough for you? Do you want to catch some whales?«

The whole wolf pack started laughing again and scoffed at Rogo.

»Whales...yeah right«, and »Whales…ha…ha.«

Then Finnomir crawled out of Rogo's fur.

»No. He is taking me there.«

The wolves fell silent and stared at Finnomir. Eratogast moved closer to Rogo and sniffed in Finnomir's direction.

»What are you?«

»My name is Finnomir and I am a butterfly.«

The big wolf sniffed again, then grimaced and gritted his teeth.

»No. Butterflies look different.«

Rogo turned his head to Finnomir and whispered:

»Crawl into my fur and hold on tight!«

The next moment the big wolf howled and the pack started to move. They circled Rogo and came closer towards him. One of them leaped forward. Rogo jumped to the side and the wolf landed where Rogo had been standing the moment before. Rogo stormed at two of the wolves and growled at them. They backed away. Then Rogo saw a shadow. He turned and looked, and in that moment Eratogast's paws landed on Rogo's body and pushed him to the ground. Rogo hit the rocks with full force and Eratogast jumped on top of him and pushed him down. With bared teeth Eratogast's snout moved slowly closer to Rogo's face. He growled:

»It's over for you now, Rogo. Once and for all.«

He opened his mouth, ready to drive his fangs into Rogo's throat, when suddenly Finnomir crawled out of the fur. He held a pine needle in his hands, and he screamed:

»Leave my friend alone!«

Using all his strength, Finnomir stabbed the pine needle right in the middle of Eratogast's nose. The big wolf backed away and howled in pain. Rogo jumped up and the two wolves faced each other and growled at each other. Eratogast rubbed his aching nose.

»You two won't get away with this. Your journey is over, here and now.«

Rogo was out of breath. He gritted his teeth grimly and growled at Eratogast.

»We will see.«

Just as Eratogast wanted to leap forward, there was a loud rumble, and out of nowhere a large, brown animal stormed onto the plateau. It was Mora the bear. She swung her paw towards the wolves and they backed away. Mora shouted:

»Rogo! Get behind me!«

Rogo leapt and stood back-to-back with Mora, facing the wolves that circled them. Then suddenly they heard the trotting of hooves, and the next moment Pito the ram came running down the plateau full speed with his head bowed. He hit the side of Eratogast's body with his horns and the big wolf was hurled through the air with full force. He landed hard on his back, but he jumped up again immediately and growled angrily:

»You're lucky this time, Rogo.«

Then Eratogast howled, and the whole pack disappeared as quickly as it had initially appeared.

*

Rogo, Mora, and Pito stood on the plateau. All three of them were out of breath. Finnomir was sitting on Rogo's shoulder and the little butterfly's face was filled with excitement and pride, and he still held the pine needle in his hand. Rogo took a deep breath of relieve, then turned to his rescuers.

»Mora, Pito, thank you. But why are you here?«

They all sat down and Mora started to explain.

»When Finnomir disappeared from the clearing, his friends were worried. Krix and Eric asked a few birds to look out for Finnomir on their flights. One of the birds came by the turtle because there are so many fat worms in the small pond. The turtle told the bird about your plan. The bird then told me. I asked Pito to join me for reinforcement and we hurried to the plateau. It looks like we came just in time.«

Rogo and Finnomir listened carefully to Mora. When they said goodbye to each other, Mora smiled at the little butterfly.

»All your friends will be waiting for you when you come flying to the clearing in the springtime, Finnomir.«

Then she turned to the wolf.

»And now to you, Rogo. We are all very proud of you and what you are doing for Finnomir. Pito and I will make sure that Eratogast leaves you alone when you come back.«

The two rescuers went down the mountain cliffs and Rogo and Finnomir watched them leave until they had disappeared, then the two travelers set off again.

*

Rogo and Finnomir hiked along a narrow path up the mountain. The world up there was made of nothing more than wet rocks covered with moss and lichen. Finnomir was sitting on Rogo's shoulder. He still had the pine needle in his hand and smiled happily. Rogo noticed.

»Why are you smiling? Didn't the wolves scare you?« Finnomir looked at his big companion and his smile became a big grin.

»They were worried about me, Eric, Krix, Mora, and Pito. I think that means they like me?«

»Of course. Why wouldn't they like you?«

»Well, because I'm different.«

»Maybe that's exactly why they like you so much, Finnomir?«

»Do you really think so?«

Rogo nodded.

»You are special, Finnomir. And you can drop the pine needle now. Eratogast's pack won't chase us up to here. Where did you conjure the needle from, by the way?«

Finnomir looked at the pine needle, then finally threw it away.

»It was in your fur. Your fur is full of this stuff. It's a good thing you don't clean yourself very often.«

Then they both laughed.

*

As they hiked higher up the mountain, they walked around the corner of a large rock and a cold wind blew suddenly in their faces. They stopped and looked up the sloping mountain side and saw the pass right ahead of them. It was covered with white powder.

»What's the white stuff up there, Rogo?«

The wolf smiled.

»That is snow, Finnomir. It is frozen water. You will like it, trust me.«

The mountain was steep and climbing over rubble and boulders was exhausting for Rogo but finally, when evening came, they reached the pass. Rogo was standing knee-deep in the snow, and Finnomir was sitting on his shoulder. A cold wind blew through the channel between the two mountain peaks and produced a soft howl. The world on the other side of the mountains was hidden under a cover of thick clouds, so thick, it gave the impression that one could just walk over them to the horizon. Above the clouds, the blue sky slowly turned red under the descending sun. Rogo took a deep breath and exhaled, and for Finnomir it sounded like his big companion was sighing at the sight of the setting sun. Rogo sniffed the air a few times.

»We will stay here for the night, Finnomir. But now you definitely want to get to know the snow, don't you?«

Finnomir smiled and nodded, and Rogo lifted him off his shoulder and set him in the snow. Finnomir immediately felt the cold under his feet and he started trudging from one foot to the other. Then he started dancing in the snow and he laughed cheerfully. Rogo watched the little butterfly amused for a while, then held out his paw.

»Come, Finnomir! Don't stay in the snow too long, or you'll catch a cold.«

Finnomir crawled up Rogo's arm onto his shoulder and Rogo took a look around.

»We need a warm place for the night. There is a cave over there, it will protect us from the cold wind.«

Rogo trudged through the snow to a small hole in the rocks, not much bigger than two of his kind would fit in. He turned around his own axis two times, then he lay down. From the small cave they saw the setting sun. They did not say a word, instead they both observed the beautiful spectacle in silence. The sun slowly dipped below the clouds and colored the sky purple until it finally became so dark that the first stars began to sparkle. Rogo curled up and Finnomir crawled into the wolf's thick fur. It was nice and warm in there. Before they fell asleep, Rogo suddenly raised his head again.

»Finnomir?«

»Yes?«

»Did you know that no butterfly has ever been as high up as you are now?«

Finnomir stuck his head out of the wolf's grey fur.

»Really?«

»Yes. You are the first to venture to such a high place.«

Finnomir blinked thoughtfully.

»Hmm. That is a nice thought.«

Then Finnomir crawled back into Rogo's fur. The wolf stuck his head in his side to protect his face from the cold and they both fell asleep to the sound of the howling wind.

The journey to the ocean

The next morning a cool gust of wind blew into the little cave and woke up the wolf. Rogo stretched cautiously, but he didn't shake like he usually did because he did not want to throw the little butterfly out of his fur. Rogo yawned, then sniffed the air a few times.

»Finnomir, are you awake?«

The little butterfly crawled out of Rogo's fur and blinked at him. Rogo smiled back.

»Good morning. We should leave immediately and reach the valley as quickly as possible.«

Finnomir rubbed his eyes.

»I'm hungry, Rogo.«

The wolf sighed.

»You have to hold out a little while longer. We must hike for half a day, then we will reach the forest in the valley on the other side. There we will find flowers.«

Finnomir crawled back into Rogo's fur to protect himself from the cold. Then they started walking. The wolf trudged through the deep snow over the mountain pass and sank almost to the shoulders with every step. The marching was arduous, and the cold wind hurt Rogo's ears and face, but he endured it bravely. After a while the mountainside went downhill, the snow slowly disappeared, and the rocky ground shone through. As the snow became more sparse, small rivulets appeared and the water splashed downhill through gravel and rock until the rivulets finally formed a small stream. Rogo stopped there.

»Finnomir, do you see the brook?«

Finnomir crawled out of Rogo's fur and looked around.

»Are there any flowers?«

»No, not yet. Be patient, Finnomir. It will not take long. We will follow this stream. It will lead us into the valley. There we will find you some flowers. I promise.«

Finnomir looked at the little brook and tried to smile. Then he crawled back under Rogo's fur and Rogo started to run. First, there was rubble everywhere, and Rogo had to be very cautious not to slip and fall but after a while the stones grew larger and finally the ground was made of solid rocks so Rogo could tread more confidently. He jumped down the mountainside from one rock to the next. At first the mountain was steep, then it became flatter and after a while, where the brook broadened, bushes and trees were growing. Rogo was panting loudly, and his long tongue hung out of his mouth. Finnomir crawled out of the fur.

»Flowers?«

The wolf looked around and sighed.

»No. Not yet, Finnomir. I'm sorry.«

Finnomir sighed too. Before he crawled back into Rogo's fur, he looked at the trees and bushes.

»The forest here looks the same as on the other side of the mountain.«

»Yes, that's true. But that will change the closer we get to the ocean, you will see.«

Rogo continued running down the mountain through the forest. He hurried as much as he could, knowing his little companion was hungry. In the forest it became warmer, so Finnomir crawled out of Rogo's fur and sat on his shoulder. It was not long before they reached the valley, and there they found a grassy area where a few flowers were growing. Rogo lifted Finnomir down and he investigated the calyx of a red flower with large blossoms. There was nectar in it and he drank until he was full.

»Ah, that was good!«

He wiped the nectar from his lips and grinned. The wolf put him back on his shoulder and while they continued walking along the stream through the forest they chatted.

»Say, Rogo?«

»Yes, Finnomir?«

»Why do the wolves know you? And why did they laugh about you eating fish?«

Rogo suddenly stopped and looked down at the pine needle covered ground. After a moment of pondering, he raised his head again and went on.

»It's a long story, Finnomir.«

»And we are on a long journey, Rogo.«

The wolf smiled and looked at the butterfly on his shoulder.

»You're a clever guy, Finnomir.«

Rogo fell silent and his face became pensive. After a few moments, he explained:

»I was once one of them. The big wolf, Eratogast, and I, we were friends a long time ago. His father was leader of the wolf pack. And when he died, Eratogast took the lead. One day we saw a group of deer in the forest; they had their newborns with them. Eratogast ordered us to chase the babies because

78

they were the easiest to catch. I refused. Then I scared off the deer so they could escape. Eratogast exiled me and I fled to the forest near the clearing. Since then I've only fed on fish from the stream.«

Then Rogo bowed his head and sighed:

»And there I am alone.«

*

Rogo and Finnomir travelled along the stream for many days. Now and then little rivulets flowed into the stream, slowly but surely turning it into a river. The river ran through a narrow valley and mountain cliffs rose on both sides. The coniferous forest soon became a deciduous forest and the valley became wider.

One day, the two travelers made their way out of the forest and suddenly they stood in a large meadow. Tall grass and colorful flowers grew there, and yellow butterflies fluttered in the air.

»Look, Finnomir! Butterflies.«

Finnomir climbed from Rogo's shoulder onto his head to get a better look. He marveled at the hustle and bustle of lemon-colored wings flapping in the air. He watched it for a moment, then he remembered the disappointing encounter with the butterfly lady in the clearing.

»Let's move on, Rogo«, he said and climbed down Rogo's shoulder again. The wolf looked at Finnomir, inquisitively.

»As you wish, Finnomir.«

Just as they were about to leave one of the yellow butterflies flew towards them and greeted them.

»Good day. You're new here, aren't you?«

Rogo stopped.

»Good afternoon to you as well. Yes, we come from the other side of the mountains.«

The yellow butterfly looked astonished.

»Oh! Really? And where are you heading to?«

»To the ocean«, Rogo said. »My little friend here is ill. There is a medical crab that lives by the ocean, he may be able to help him.«

The butterfly flew around Finnomir and looked at him closely, but Finnomir was not comfortable with being watched, so he turned his face to the side as though he was ashamed. The yellow butterfly circled Finnomir once in flight, then hovered in the air before him.

»Ah, now I see it. You are one of the butterflies with purple and blue wings, but your wings have not grown properly, am I right?«

Finnomir bowed his head and the butterfly noticed Finnomir's sadness.

»Oh! I'm so sorry. I did not mean to offend you. By the way, my name is *Siddak*. And what is your name?«

Finnomir looked up at Siddak who fluttered up and down in the air.

»I am Finnomir and I want to be able to fly like you. That's why my friend is taking me to the ocean. The medical crab may be able to heal my wings.«

The yellow butterfly nodded in agreement.

»Definitely, Finnomir. I've heard many amazing stories about this crab. There was a fox with an injured leg. The crab healed his leg and he could walk again. I also heard of a bird with a broken wing. He too was healed and was able to fly again. If anyone can help you, Finnomir, it will be this crab.«

When Finnomir heard this, he started smiling.

»Is that true?«

»Yes. At least that is what I have heard.«

Finnomir and Rogo looked at each other and smiled, then Rogo turned to the hovering butterfly.

»This is good news, Siddak. Thank you.«

Siddak bowed while hovering in the air.

»My pleasure. No need to thank me.«

Rogo looked at the river. Then he looked to the horizon.

»Oh, Siddak? Do you know how far it is to the ocean?«

»Yes. If you follow this river, you will see the ocean in about three weeks.«

»Three weeks?«, Rogo said in astonishment.

»Well, if that's the case, we'd better hurry up.«

Then they said goodbye. The yellow butterfly wished Finnomir all the best and the two travelers moved on. They walked through a meadow of tall grass along the riverbank while Finnomir sat on Rogo's shoulder and smiled.

»You know what, Rogo?«

»What, Finnomir?«

»When I will be able to fly, I might even fly faster than you can run.«

Rogo laughed, amused.

>>We'll see, Finnomir.<<

Then Rogo stopped.

>>Finnomir, would you like to test what it's like to fly?<<
>>How would that work?<<
>>Climb on my head and hold on to my hair.<<

Finnomir did it. He was sitting on Rogo's forehead just above his eyebrows and he grabbed a tuft of fur on the left and right. Then he asked:

>>What now?<<
>>Hold on tight!<<, said Rogo.

Then Rogo started to run. He picked up speed and galloped faster and faster across the meadow along the bank of the river. Finnomir felt the wind brush around his body and he had to hold on tight to keep from falling off Rogo's head. The wolf had run fast before, but this was different. Before now the forest was too dense and the terrain was too impassable for high speeds but on this meadow there were no obstacles, and Rogo ran like the wind. Finnomir saw the world whizzing past him. It really felt as though he was flying through the air and he laughed with joy and shouted:

»Hooray!«

Rogo laughed loudly too as he raced through the meadow, and he felt in his heart that Finnomir was happy.

*

They had left behind the meadow with the yellow butterflies a week ago, and they were still following the river that curled through the valley like a snake. The further they travelled, the wider the valley became, but that was not the only thing that had changed. The air was warmer and humid. Rogo noticed it when he was getting hotter than usual when he ran. A few days later Finnomir felt it too. He no longer crawled under Rogo's fur because it got so hot that he almost could not breathe. The plants looked different too. The trees became scarcer, the flowers became more colorful, and the grass was growing taller. Soon Rogo had to raise his head to look over the meadow. On one hot day the valley narrowed again and a cliff blocked the travelers' path. The wolf was looking for a way to climb over the rock, but it was too steep. He looked up at the grey wall, helplessly.

»We can't go on here, Finnomir.«

The butterfly climbed on Rogo's head and looked around.

»What should we do now, Rogo?«

The wolf looked at the riverbank and there he saw a way out.

»Look over there, Finnomir. A tree trunk. It has fallen across the river.«

Rogo went to the tree log and inspected it carefully.

»A storm probably knocked the tree over, and now it forms a bridge. This is our way out. Here we can cross the river. Over there, there is no cliff that blocks our way, and we can continue our journey on the other side.«

Finnomir looked at the tree trunk and he noticed how old and rotten the wood was.

»It doesn't look very safe to me, Rogo.«

The wolf pawed the tree trunk and tried to wiggle it, but it didn't move. He smiled confidently.

»It'll be fine. We have no other option anyway.«

Rogo carefully took a few steps onto the tree trunk.

»Seems to be stable so far.«

Finnomir didn't answer, instead he stared anxiously at the roaring river below their feet. Then Rogo took a few steps forward and the round trunk wobbled a little bit. Finnomir cried out in fear.

»Careful!«

The little butterfly's heart was beating out of his chest and he clutched at Rogo's hair. The wolf moved forward, step by step, one paw at a time and he elegantly balanced on the tree trunk that was wobbling beneath his feet. They had finally reached the middle of the river, and below them the gushing water roared so loudly that it deafened their ears. Therefore, neither of them heard the wood crunching beneath them, but Rogo could feel it in his paws and his movement froze in terror. For a moment he thought the trip to the ocean would end here and now for both of them, but the crunching under his feet stopped. He wondered if he might be able to jump to the other bank, but in that very moment a loud cracking sound drowned the noise of the river and the tree gave way. The rotten log broke into two pieces and Rogo no longer felt a solid hold beneath his paws.

»Hold on, Finnomir! We are falling!«

With a loud splash, they plunged into the river. The water was freezing cold and the current was wild. The wolf was spun around and up and down. He tried to swim, but he was thrown around by the raging water like a little twig. Then Rogo felt something firm underneath his paws. It was the broken tree trunk. He clutched the round piece of wood and managed to keep his head over water. He yelled:

»Finnomir! Are you still here?«

The little butterfly was still sitting on Rogo's head, holding firmly onto his fur. He spat water.

»Yes. I'm still here, Rogo.«

Holding on to the floating piece of wood they drifted along the river for hours. The current was fast and furious until the water finally slowed down and the log was washed up against a sandbar and Rogo jumped off the tree and onto the riverbank. He lifted Finnomir down and set him on the grass, then he shook his fur violently, as if he wanted to shake away all the tension and all the fear together with the drops of water, leaving behind a sense of relief.

»We made it!«, he said looking out over the river where he saw the log come loose from the sandbar to continue on its journey on the river without the two travelers.

For a while, the two sat in silence in the sun to dry themselves and they were staring out at the river, then Rogo took a deep breath and sighed.

»I thought I might have to use the medical crab's

services too.«

Finnomir stared at Rogo with a horrified look in his eyes.

»And I thought we wouldn't need the crab's service anymore at all!«

They both broke out in laughter. It was not so much a laughter of joy, but they were laughing with relief. After a while, the wolf stood up and walked down to the river bed.

»What are you doing, Rogo?«

The wolf looked back at Finnomir.

»I'm hungry and there is fish in the river.«

Finnomir's eyes widened as if he had just had a brilliant idea.

»Oh! Food. That's a good idea.«

And while Rogo caught a fish, Finnomir climbed onto the next flower and drank the nectar from its goblet.

After a while they were dry again and they were full. Dusk was falling so they decided to stay there for the night. Finnomir found a place with soft moss to sleep in, and Rogo huddled next to Finnomir. They slept soundly all night long, which was no wonder after the strain of their wild adventure. The next morning they moved on.

*

The days passed by, and the closer they came to the ocean the more the landscape continued to change. Soon, there were no trees at all, and after a while the world was only covered by meadows. They turned around and looked back in the direction they came from. They looked at the snow-capped mountain peaks in the far distance and marveled at how far they had already hiked, but eventually even the mountain peaks were no longer visible. The grass in this part of the world grew short, and the green of the leaves turned lighter as they travelled further along the river, but there were still enough flowers for Finnomir to drink from.

They had been on the move for weeks now, and the river had become so wide that ten tree trunks would not have been enough to cross over it. The wolf suddenly stopped and held his nose up in the air.

»What's the matter, Rogo?«

Rogo sniffed excitedly and his nose was wiggling up and down.

»I smell something.«

Then he looked at Finnomir and smiled.

»Hold on tight!«

Rogo started to run. He ran straight to the horizon where the grass suddenly ended and was replaced by sand dunes. Rogo climbed onto one of the dunes and stopped. Stretched out in front of the two travelers there was this infinite pond the turtle had spoken of. Rogo's chest rose and fell and he sighed, as if his heart was aching with joy and awe.

»We're here, Finnomir! This is the ocean. We finally made it!«

Finnomir sat on Rogo's shoulder, and he was speechless. He stared at the great blue water that stretched out before him. It seemed to have no end. Just like Rogo, Finnomir was overwhelmed by this feeling in his chest; a feeling that was intense but joyful.

»Yes Rogo, we made it«, he said softly.

Then they sat on the dune and looked at the endless waters. A light wind blew from the shore and cooled the two hikers who had come from the forest on the other side of the mountains. They watched the waves towering up far out in the ocean, with foaming edges, rushing towards the mainland with a loud roar, overturning and collapsing before they reached the shore, until they finally ran gently onto the beach, wet the sand and retreated to make room for the next wave to come. Finnomir looked at Rogo and he recognized the awe and enthusiasm in his expression. Then he looked out at the ocean and smiled.

»How wonderful that I am able to witness this.«

The ocean

Rogo stood up to his knees in the water and stared down at the ocean floor. He had already caught one fish today, but a second one would not be bad either. The fish in the ocean tasted a little different than the fish in the streams of the forest, but they tasted just as good, especially when one was hungry.

Finnomir was sitting on a stone by a dune at a safe distance, watching the wolf. Rogo had not moved in several minutes. Only his head sometimes moved back and forth with short, jerky movements and each time Finnomir thought a fish was swimming past Rogo's legs and he waited for Rogo to pounce on one, grab it in his mouth and hurl it out of the water onto the shore. But that didn't happen.

*

As Finnomir watched the wolf, his mind wandered. They had been at the ocean for three days now, but they had not yet found the medical crab. They had followed the river from the mountains to the place where the river poured into the ocean. They had the river on their left, so they could not go in that direction. They had no choice but to move in the other direction, with the ocean on the left and the dunes on their right. Finnomir was worried they might be on the wrong side and he asked the wolf about it but Rogo just said they would find a way. Now that they have come this far, the rest of the journey could not be that difficult. But Finnomir recognized the concern in Rogo's voice.

*

Rogo suddenly moved, but it was not his typical fishing move. He just turned and waded out of the water. This brought Finnomir's thoughts back to the present. The wolf ran to the sand dune, then shook his fur dry and sat next to Finnomir.

»One fish will have to be enough today«, he sighed.

»I'm sorry«, Finnomir replied.

Rogo smiled at the butterfly.

»It doesn't matter.«

They sat there staring at the ocean for a while, then Rogo stood up and held out his paw to Finnomir.

»We should move on.«

Finnomir nodded. He climbed up Rogo's arm, sat on his

94

shoulder and they continued their journey. They walked along the beach until afternoon, when Finnomir became hungry. The wolf climbed over the sand dunes and they travelled inland. There were meadows with flowers, and Finnomir drank nectar from them. Then they went back to the beach and when they stood on a dune and looked out at the ocean, they discovered something strange. Far out in the sea, where the waves were high, a group of big fish jumped out of the water into the air. The fish giggled strangely, and their noises could be heard even though they were so far away. Whenever they jumped out of the water, they did somersaults and then splashed back into the water. It appeared they were having a lot of fun. A couple of the big fish stuck their heads out of the water and it looked as if they were talking to each other. Then one of them nodded towards the bank, as if to point to the wolf and the butterfly. The other fish also nodded as if they agreed, then they giggled, swam away, and left one big fish alone. The fish stared at the bank and it all seemed strange to Finnomir.

»Do you see the big fish out there, Rogo?«

»Yes. He and his friends were watching us.«

Just as Rogo had said this, the big fish swam straight towards them. He came into the shallow waters right in front of the dune. He stuck his head out of the water and giggled.

»Hello guys! You're new here, aren't you?«

Rogo and Finnomir looked at each other in amazement.

»The fish can talk!«, said Rogo.

»I'm not a fish«, replied the fish. »Why don't you two come closer to the water so we can talk? I cannot go ashore.«

Rogo stood up and walked to the shore with Finnomir on his shoulder. They stopped there. Two steps in front of them, the strange, speaking fish held his head over the waterline and grinned at them. He had a long mouth, almost like a bird's beak. Rogo greeted the big fish.

»Good day. Who are you? If you are not a fish, what are you?«

The big fish giggled.

»I am a dolphin and I'm a mammal.«

»A dolphin?«, Finnomir asked in surprise.

»Yes. My name is *Didu*.«

Rogo scratched his ear, looking a little confused.

»I am Rogo. I am a wolf. The butterfly on my shoulder is named Finnomir.«

Didu giggled again.

»Greetings to you.«

Rogo sat down on the sand. Then he asked:

»Didu, what do dolphins do all day?«

Didu nodded his head up and down quickly and he made sounds like a chatter.

»We swim around and explore the world. We eat fish and jump out of the water just for fun.«

»You are exploring the world?«, asked Finnomir.

»Yes«, Didu replied. »Did you know that the world is a big blue ball? It is blue because it is largely covered with water. This ball races through space terribly quickly, always in a circle around the sun.«

Rogo and Finnomir looked blankly at Didu.

»What is space?«, Finnomir asked.

Didu giggled.

»It's the empty void between the stars.«

»I don't understand«, said Finnomir, a little disappointed.

»It doesn't matter«, Didu replied. »Many animals do not understand.«

Rogo looked up at the cloudless sky and pondered. Then he

turned back to the dolphin.

»Say Didu, what's on the other side of this ball?«

The dolphin giggled again.

»Another continent.«

»A continent? What is that?«

»It's a mainland. Like the one you're sitting on right now, my dear wolf.«

Rogo looked at the sandy floor under his feet. Then he and Finnomir looked at each other puzzled.

»Do animals live on this other continent as well?«, Finnomir asked.

»Of course«, Didu replied. »Not long ago I swam to the other side of the ball and got to know the animals there. Well, at least the ones I could talk to from the shallow water at the beach. The amazing thing was that the animals there didn't know anything about our continent either. Just as neither of you knew anything about the other continents until today.«

»You just said continents. Are there any more?«, Finnomir interposed.

Didu quickly nodded his head up and down.

»Oh yes. Three or four continents. Maybe more. I do

98

not know for sure, because I have not explored the whole blue ball yet.«

The dolphin dove under water and briefly swam in a circle. He blew water from a hole in the top of his head. Then he swam back to them.

»Tell me now my wolf and butterfly friends. Where are you two coming from? I have never seen you here before.«

Rogo pointed back over his shoulder.

»We come from the forest at the other side of the mountains.«

The dolphin stuck his head out of the water and tried to look across the dunes.

»Mountains? What are mountains?«

»Mountains are rocks so high that they touch the clouds.«

Didu opened his mouth wide and stared at Rogo in amazement.

»They touch the clouds? Really?«

»Yes, the mountain tips reach up to the clouds.«

»That's incredible«, Didu said in astonishment. »And your forest is there beyond those mountains?«

Rogo and Finnomir nodded at the same time. Then Didu asked

further:

»And what's the name of your forest?«

Rogo and Finnomir looked at each other a bit clueless, then Finnomir answered the dolphin:

»The forest has no name. It's just *the forest*.«

Didu stared at them with an open mouth. Then he dipped his head under water and sprayed a fountain out of the hole in his head, as he had done before.

»Well, then you have probably come a long way. May I ask why you came to the ocean?«

»It's because of my wings«, said Finnomir. »They are too small and I am unable to fly with them. I heard of a medical crab that lives by the ocean. He might be able to heal my wings.«

Didu nodded his head up and down excitedly.

»Yes, oh yes, the crab lives here! And I know where you can find him.«

»Really?!«, Finnomir exclaimed.

»Yes«, said Didu. »But you're on the wrong side of the river.«

Finnomir's happy expression instantly disappeared.

100

»That's exactly what I was afraid of, Rogo.«

Rogo sighed and shook his head in disappointment. Then he looked at Didu.

»Do you know a way to the other side?«

Didu giggled as if the whole thing was funny. He stuck his body out of the water and began to dance around on the water with powerful strokes of his tail fin.

»Of course! I can help you get there. Dolphins always like to help. I will take you to the other side.«

Rogo and Finnomir looked at each other in confusion.

»How would that work, Didu?«, Finnomir asked.

»Well, it's very simple. You sit on the wolf, just like you do now, and the wolf will stand on my back. Then I'll carry you to the other side of the river mouth.« He giggled again. »I'm just piggybacking you. That's an easy task for me.«

Rogo stood up and looked out at the ocean nervously. He looked at the high waves, then he looked at Didu and shook his head.

»I don't think that's a good idea. You should know, we already had an unpleasant experience with a wild river on our journey here. We almost drowned.«

Finnomir pulled Rogo by the fur.

»But we survived, didn't we? And we will survive this too. I trust the dolphin. Besides, we have no other choice. We somehow have to get to the other side.«

Rogo looked pensive and unsure, maybe even a little scared. He saw the endless ocean in front of him, and he was not at all comfortable with the thought of riding over wild giant waves on the back of a large fish that is not a fish. But Finnomir was right. They had no other choice. So, Rogo stomped out into the water. Didu swam as close to the bank as he could, but the wolf still got wet up to his shoulders. Finnomir had climbed up Rogo's head for safety. Then Rogo climbed onto Didu's back. At first, he had a queasy feeling. But he quickly realized that the dolphin underneath his feet was much more stable than the old tree trunk at the river. Didu suddenly whizzed away. He tried to make sure that his passengers weren't sprayed too much but that was in vain. When Didu tried to swim over a big wave as carefully as possible, a gush of water splashed over his head and hit Rogo in the face. Finnomir got wet too. But unlike Rogo, Finnomir found the whole experience fun and he laughed out loud and asked:

»Isn't that wonderful, Rogo!?«

Rogo snorted and blew the water out of his nose.

»I have mixed feelings, Finnomir. I long to go ashore.«
Didu giggled.

»I'm sorry, but there was no other way around this wave.«

It was not long before they reached the other side of the river mouth.

»I have to get you ashore here«, Didu said.

»Is the crab here?«, Finnomir asked.

»No, my little friend. The crab lives a little further up the coast but I can't swim there. There are big waves and dangerous rocks. It will not be a problem on foot and you will find the crab soon, you will see.«

Didu swam up to the bank at a place where the water was shallow. Rogo dismounted Didu and was startled because the water suddenly reached up to his neck. He stuck his head out of the water and quickly waded to the shore and finally reached the dry beach.

»Are you still here, Finnomir?«

»Yes«, said Finnomir cheerfully, but also a little exhausted from the exciting ride on the dolphin. »Yes, Rogo. I am still here.«

Then they stood on the beach and looked at Didu. He swam out into the deeper waters, nodded his head up and down and giggled:

»Just a little further up the coast. There you will find the crab.«

Then he turned and while swimming away he shouted:

»Goodbye, my foreign friends. Good luck to you.«

»Thank you for your help«, Finnomir called after the dolphin. They watched Didu jump over a big wave, then he dived under water and was gone.

The medical crab

Finnomir and Rogo walked along the beach in the direction Didu had shown them, and Finnomir was sitting on Rogo's shoulder. Now that they were on the right side of the estuary, it shouldn't be hard to find the medical crab. Soon evening came and they were looking for a place to sleep somewhere inland behind the dunes. Finnomir drank nectar from a flower for dinner, and he particularly enjoyed the sweet meal that evening. He pulled his head out of the calyx and grinned. His mouth was smeared with nectar and he wiped it off.

»Do you think we'll find the crab tomorrow, Rogo?«

Rogo pawed the tall grass for a place to sleep. Then he turned twice in a circle and lay down. He yawned loudly and put his head on his paws.

»It is quite possible. Now that we're on the right side, it's probably just a matter of time. Didu said it wasn't far.«

Finnomir smiled confidently. Then he climbed down from the flower and picked up two large leaves. He lay on top of one and covered himself with the other. It was dusk and not dark yet, but the exciting day had made Finnomir very tired and so he closed his eyes. Just before he fell asleep, he muttered to himself:

»Tomorrow. The crab. Perhaps tomorrow.«

Rogo was watching Finnomir. It made Rogo happy to see that the little butterfly was in a good mood. He waited for the moon to rise. Then Rogo also became tired and fell asleep.

*

The next morning, they left early and hiked along the rocky coast. They weren't on the road for long, when Rogo suddenly stopped.

»Look over there, Finnomir! There are seagulls sitting on a rock. Maybe we should ask them.«

When the two reached the rock, the seagulls were startled at the sight of the wolf and fluttered up in a fuss. Rogo called after them:

»Wait! I mean no harm.«

One seagull fluttered over Rogo's head, high enough that Rogo would never reach her even with a giant leap. The seagull croaked:

»Who are you and what do you want?«

Rogo pointed at Finnomir, who was sitting on his shoulder.

»My friend needs help. We are looking for the medical crab. Do you know where we can find him?«

The gull took a close look at Finnomir, then she realized that the two strangers were no danger. She croaked:

»I know the way.«

She flew ahead and Rogo followed her. The seagull flew along the beach for a while, then sat on a rock covered with green and brown algae. She pointed at a cave.

»Here we are. You will find the crab inside this cave.«

Then she fluttered up and flew away. Rogo and Finnomir looked at the entrance of the cave. It had the shape of a crack in the rock that ran from top to bottom becoming wider and rounder towards the ground. The roar of the surf echoed inside the cave. Finnomir started to tremble.

»I'm scared, Rogo.«

The wolf calmed Finnomir.

»Courage, my little friend. We have come this far. We won't be put off by a dark cave.«

107

He said it, and went inside.

It was cold inside the cave. Only a few rays of sunlight fell from little cracks and holes in the rocky ceiling. And surprisingly, inside the cave the echo of the surf was not as loud and terrifying as suspected. A strange *clip clap* sound came from a corner of the cave. They looked in the direction of the sound, and they saw a crab sitting on a stone, cutting seaweed into small pieces. The crab had turned its back to them and didn't notice the two strangers, so Rogo went closer and greeted the crab.

»Good day, Sir«, he said.

The crab was startled and spun around quickly, raising his pincers as if to defend himself. Rogo took a step back.

»Don't be scared! We won't harm you. We are seeking help from the famous medical crab. Did we come to the right place?«

The crab opened one pair of pincers just a little and peeked through the crack with one of his eyes.

»Who is we?«, the crab asked.

»I am Rogo. And the little butterfly on my shoulder is Finnomir.«

Finnomir smiled gently and waved to the crab.

»Good day.«

The crab lowered his pincers and looked at Finnomir curiously.

»Oh!?«, he said in astonishment. Then he waved at Finnomir.

»Come down to me, little butterfly. I want to take a closer look at you.«

Rogo lifted the butterfly down and sat him on the rock by the crab.

»Your name is Finnomir, you say?«

Finnomir nodded and the crab waved his pincers in a circle.

»Please turn around so I can examine your wings more closely!«

Finnomir did so and the crab examined Finnomir. He unfolded his wings and asked:

»Does that hurt?«

»No«, Finnomir replied.

Then the crab pulled Finnomir's wings up and down and to the sides, and asked again whether it hurt. But Finnomir felt nothing. When the crab finished the examination, he scratched his chin and shook his head.

»Well, Finnomir. You have the butterfly disease, no question about that, but I don't think I can help you. You feel nothing at all in your wings. This means there is no life in them anymore. There is nothing left that could be healed.«

Finnomir stared at the crab in horror without saying a word, then he looked desperately at Rogo. Rogo saw the helplessness in Finnomir's eyes, and this made him very sad, so he turned to the crab.

»But we heard about a fox with an injured leg that you healed.«

The crab shook his head.

»The fox just had a splinter in his paw. I pulled it out with my pincers. That was all.«

Rogo contemplated for a moment.

»But what about the bird with the broken wing?«

»I put a splint on his wing and the fracture healed on its own«, the crab replied.

Rogo was desperate.

»But can't you do anything at all to help Finnomir? We have come from the other side of the mountains and we have been traveling for many weeks hoping you could heal

Finnomir's wings.«

The crab scratched his head and contemplated for a while.

»Well, maybe the salamander slime might help. But this method has never been tested on butterflies.«

Finnomir turned to the crab and looked curiously.

»Salamander slime?«

»Yes. A special type of salamander lives here in this very cave. If they hurt themselves, everything heals on its own. Their skin secretes a sticky mucus, and I've already tested it on minor injuries on different animals. Unfortunately, it does not work with all kinds of animals. The slime of the salamander has had a very good effect on an injured turtle. I was also able to heal a small wound on a pelican. But with crabs like me, the slime doesn't work at all. We can try the slime for therapy, Finnomir. But I can't make any promises.«

Finnomir was silent. He just stood there and thought for a moment. Then he looked at Rogo, who immediately nodded wildly in agreement, so Finnomir turned back to the crab.

»Okay then. I want to try it, because otherwise I will have travelled all this way for nothing.«

The crab smiled.

»Very well, Finnomir. Wait here!«

Then the crab went to get the slime.

*

Only a short while later, Finnomir got his first pack of sticky salamander slime smeared on his wings. The slime smelt awful, but Finnomir did not care. Then he walked along the beach with Rogo and they found a cozy place behind a sand dune. There was grass and a few flowers from which Finnomir could drink the nectar. They sat down and rested, and for a while they were silent. Then they started chatting.

»I wonder what's going on in the clearing now?«, Finnomir asked.

»It's autumn«, said Rogo, in an almost wistful voice, as if he was homesick. »The leaves first turn red then brown and finally they fall from the trees. The hedgehogs eat their fill and prepare for hibernation. Most birds are already on their way to the warm winter quarters in the south. It won't be long before it starts to snow and the forest and the clearing will be entirely covered in white.«

»Will it snow here as well, Rogo?«

The wolf shook his head.

»No. It's too warm here by the ocean and that's a good thing. Otherwise you wouldn't find flowers with nectar to drink from.«

Then evening fell. They sat on the dune and watched the sunset before they went to sleep. The next morning Finnomir woke up and he felt something strange. He became frightened.

»Rogo! Rogo! Wake up!«

The wolf opened his eyes in alarm and looked at Finnomir with concern.

»What's wrong, Finnomir?«

Finnomir pointed to his back.

»My wings, Rogo. They are tingling.«

The wolf rubbed his eyes.

»They are doing what?«

»I feel a tingling in my wings. I don't know if that's good or bad. I want to go to the crab right away.«

»Very well«, said Rogo.

He put Finnomir on his shoulder and ran to the crab's cave. The crab was taking his morning bath in a puddle of water and

Finnomir excitedly told him the news. The crab climbed out of the bath and examined Finnomir's wings.

»The tingling could be a good sign, Finnomir«, said the crab. »Perhaps the slime actually works on you.«

Finnomir's eyes lit up with joy, and immediately the crab gave him the next pack of slime. Finnomir was happy. He had high hopes that the treatment could work and that he would fly home on his own with healed wings.

*

Finnomir was treated with the slime for two weeks, during which time he went on an excursion with Rogo every day. They walked along the beach, explored every sand dune, turned rocks, and checked what was hidden beneath. At lunchtime, Rogo caught fish and Finnomir drank nectar from a flower. Then they always sat on the same big rock and watched the ocean. Sometimes they saw a few dolphins jumping over waves, making their strange noises, and they wondered if Didu was there too.

*

One morning Finnomir woke up and found something strange in his bed. It looked like a piece of a dried leaf. He picked it up, looked at it, and showed it to the wolf.

»Rogo, look! What is that?«

The wolf had a worrying idea about what it might be, but he did not tell Finnomir.

»We should show it to the crab, Finnomir.«

They went to the cave and the crab examined Finnomir's wings and the strange piece he had brought with him. Then the crab sighed.

»I'm sorry, Finnomir. The therapy does not work. A piece of your wing has broken off, and more pieces will break off in the next few weeks until at some point none of your wings will be left.«

Finnomir froze and looked at the crab in horror and a terrible pain arose in his chest. He stared at the piece of broken wing in his hands for a while, then he just dropped it and looked down at it on the ground for a moment. All his hope was gone in one fell swoop. Without raising his head, he said:

»Thank you for your troubles, dear crab.«

Then he turned and looked at the wolf.

»Please take me home, Rogo!«

The wolf didn't say anything. He too was very sad. He just nodded and put Finnomir on his shoulder and they started their journey back home.

The journey home

Finnomir was sitting on Rogo's shoulder and they walked upstream along the river bank. At noon they took a break. Rogo put Finnomir on the grass and he drank nectar. The wolf looked back towards the ocean in the distance, he raised his nose and sniffed.

»I can't smell the ocean anymore. I think we have left it behind for good.«

Finnomir sat on a flower petal and looked in the opposite direction, towards home.

»How long will it take to get home, Rogo?«

Rogo shrugged his shoulders.

»Just as long as it took us to get to the ocean, Finnomir.«

Then he sat down next to the butterfly.

»It is now winter at home and everything is covered in snow. When we arrive at the clearing it will be spring. It's still warm here on this side of the mountains and there are enough flowers for you to drink on our journey home.«

Finnomir looked down thoughtfully.

»Well, some good news at least.«

»What do you mean?«

Finnomir shrugged.

»Nothing. Let's move on.«

Rogo lifted Finnomir up on his shoulder and they continued walking until evening. When the moon rose, they looked for a cozy place to sleep in the tall grass. Rogo flattened the long stalks of grass with his paws to prepare for his night's rest. He lay down and Finnomir climbed up a long blade of grass.

»What are you doing, Finnomir?«

»I want to see the moon.«

Rogo looked up at the bright disc in the sky.

»Beautiful, isn't it?«

Finnomir stood on the tip of the wobbling blade of grass and stared at the moon.

»Yes. The moon really is beautiful. I've never noticed that before.«

He climbed down from the blade of grass again and sat next to Rogo.

»I'm looking forward to seeing my friends again. Krix will have to tell me an awful lot of news.«

Rogo put his chin on his paws and sighed.

»Yes. Friends.«

Then they both fell asleep.

*

It was the next morning. Rogo opened his eyes and saw Finnomir standing in the grass. He had turned his back on him, but Rogo saw that Finnomir was holding something in his hands and was staring at it.

»What have you got there, Finnomir?«

Finnomir turned around and held up the item so Rogo could see it.

»A piece of my wings has broken off again.«

Rogo looked at the small fragment.

»I'm really sorry, Finnomir. Is there anything I can do for you?«

Finnomir tried to conjure a smile and shook his head.

»No. I just want to go home. That is my only wish.«

He dropped the broken piece of his wing to the ground and

looked down at it for a few moments. Then he looked around and spotted a colorful flower. He climbed up and drank its nectar. Then he was refreshed and they moved on.

*

They hiked upstream along the river for many days. Every morning a broken piece of Finnomir's wings lay in his bed. For the first few days, he kept picking up the fragment and looking at it closely, but one day he just left it unheeded. Rogo saw Finnomir's wings shrink with each passing day, and at the same time Finnomir's strength was waning. He crawled under Rogo's fur and slept there for most of the time. Only when they had a rest did he crawl out for Rogo to put him in the meadow so he could climb a flower to drink nectar.

One day they reached the place where they wanted to cross the river and plunged into the roaring stream. Rogo stopped there.

»Finnomir, look!«

Finnomir crawled out of the fur and he looked tired. He blinked and examined the place until he remembered.

»Oh. Here we fell into the river, didn't we?«

»Yes. Exactly.«

The wolf smiled and pointed upstream.

»Look a bit further!«

Finnomir climbed on Rogo's head and then he saw it.

»The mountains!«, he called out excitedly. »There is the forest and the foot of the mountains. Have we actually come this far?«

Rogo felt Finnomir's happiness.

»Yes, Finnomir. Maybe two more weeks and you'll be home again.«

»Home«, he answered wistfully. Then he looked at the river.

»But, Rogo? Don't we have to cross the river?«

Rogo shook his head.

»No. As long as there are no obstacles in our way, we can hike along this side of the river. Further upstream, the river becomes a narrow stream anyway, so that we can cross it on foot.«

Then Rogo looked up at the sky.

»It will be dark soon. We should look for a place to

spend the night. There is a group of trees in the middle of the meadow. Let's go there.«

They went to the trees and set up camp there. Finnomir was too weak to climb a flower, so Rogo lifted him up on a petal, and after Finnomir drank a mouthful, the wolf placed him next to a tree trunk.

»Here is soft moss, Finnomir.«

Finnomir lay down and Rogo picked a leaf and used it to cover Finnomir. The butterfly looked at Rogo wearily and said softly:

»Thank you, Rogo.«

Then he turned on his side and fell asleep immediately.

*

After a while Finnomir was woken up by a strange sound. It was still night and the stars shone brightly in the sky. He pushed the leaf aside, sat upright, and leaned back against the tree trunk. Rogo was lying a few steps away and slept soundly. Suddenly there was the strange sound again.

»*Caw! Caw!*«

Finnomir looked up. A raven sat on a thick branch in the tree right above Finnomir's head, staring down at him.

»*Caw!* Where are you going, Finnomir? Where are you going?«

Finnomir rubbed his tired eyes.

»How do you know my name?«

The raven flapped his wings, flew up and sat on a lower branch that was closer to Finnomir.

»Your name? Your name? *Caw!* I know all the names there are. All the names. *Caw!*«

Finnomir looked at the bird suspiciously and pointed at Rogo.

»Then what's the name of the wolf?«

The raven looked at the sleeping wolf and contemplated for a moment.

»The name of the wolf? The wolf is called wolf. *Caw!*«

Then he giggled cheekily and strutted back and forth on the branch. Finnomir looked at Rogo and shouted:

»Rogo! Wake up!«

Rogo didn't move and the raven on the branch giggled again.

»He can't hear you. Let him sleep. Sleepy sleep. *Caw!*«

Finnomir felt nervous, but he did not show his fear.

»What do you want from me you weird bird?«

The raven opened his beak and cocked his head.

»I want nothing from you, nothing from you. *Caw!* I will accompany you for a while and visit you three times, three times. *Caw!*«

»And why?«, Finnomir asked.

»*Caw!* You want to go home, right?«

»Yes, I do. And?«

»*Caw!* What's home, Finnomir?«

Finnomir didn't quite understand what the raven was getting at.

»Well. Home is where I live. Home is where I come from. Home is the forest, the clearing, the big tree in the middle. All of that.«

»*Caw!* What's waiting for you there, Finnomir?«

Finnomir shrugged and thought for a moment.

»Well, my friends, of course. Krix the grasshopper, Eric the mouse and all the other animals in the clearing.«

The raven cocked his head again.

»And what is waiting for the wolf? Friends as well?

Caw!«

Finnomir looked thoughtfully at the sleeping wolf. He knew how lonely Rogo had been all alone in the forest.

»I don't think he has any friends other than me.«

The raven flapped his wings a few times, then he nodded towards the wolf.

»Friends for the wolf. That is your task, Finnomir. Your task. *Caw!*«

Then the raven pushed himself off the branch and flew away and Finnomir watched the weird bird quickly disappear into the darkness of the night. Then he thought about Rogo. It made him sad to know that Rogo had no friends other than him.

»I'll have to do something about this«, he thought. »I hope I still have enough time.«

Then Finnomir fell asleep again.

*

It was the next morning. Rogo stood in front of Finnomir and sniffed him.

»Finnomir, wake up!«

Finnomir opened his eyes and noticed Rogo's concerned facial expression.

»What's the matter, Rogo?«

Rogo took a deep breath of relief.

»I've been trying to wake you up for five minutes, but you haven't moved a bit.«

Finnomir rubbed his eyes and yawned.

»I did not sleep well. A raven woke me up last night and talked to me.«

Rogo looked at Finnomir in disbelief.

»A raven you say? But I did not hear anything.«

»I know. You slept soundly. I called for you, but you didn't react at all.«

Rogo looked surprised and scratched his ear with his paw.

»That's strange. I'm usually a light sleeper and I used to wake up at the slightest disturbance.«

Finnomir pushed the leaf aside and slowly got up.

»It doesn't matter, Rogo. Could you please bring me a flower with nectar? I do not feel well this morning. I do not think I can climb a stalk.«

»Of course, Finnomir.«

Then Rogo plucked a flower for his little friend so he could drink nectar.

*

They continued their journey upstream along the river that ran through the forest. The closer they came to the mountains the narrower the river became until finally it turned into a small stream. Now they could cross through the water easily and continue their journey on the other side.

After a few days they reached the base of the mountains. It was already evening and so they prepared their night camp. Finnomir had been very weak for days, and Rogo was increasingly worried about him. But he said nothing. He didn't want to worry the little butterfly. Rogo picked a flower and brought it to Finnomir so he could drink nectar. But Finnomir only took a sip.

»You have to drink more, Finnomir.«

Finnomir smiled at Rogo, but his smile was weak and his eyes looked exhausted.

»I've had enough, my dear Rogo. I am tired and I want

to sleep.«

Rogo sighed.

»All right. But promise me you'll drink a little more tomorrow.«

Finnomir smiled.

»I'll try.«

Then Finnomir lay down on a patch of moss and fell asleep immediately. Rogo picked a leaf from a tree and covered Finnomir with it. Then he stood in front of the little butterfly for a few moments, watching him sleep. He was worried. Finnomir's wings were almost completely gone. Little pieces of it broke off every day. As the wings continued to crumble, Finnomir grew weaker and more tired. He slept most of the time in Rogo's fur as the wolf hurried to get to the clearing as quickly as possible so Finnomir could finally be home. Rogo was at a loss. He thought: *What will the animals of the forest think when they learn that Finnomir has not been cured.* He was very afraid of that day. Rogo sighed, then he curled up close next to Finnomir and fell asleep.

*

A voice called in the distance:

»Attention! Attention! Landing approach. *Caw!*«

Finnomir woke up. Moonlight shimmered through the treetops, and something moved in the dim light.

»*Caw!* Watch out!«

Finnomir recognized the raven immediately. He flew through the gaps in the treetops and headed straight for the tree where Finnomir was sitting. The raven tried to slow down his flight by flapping his wings violently.

»Oh oh! This will be a crash-landing, ... *Aaaahhh!*«

With his face and chest, the raven crashed against the tree trunk, then he fell straight to the ground and remained lying on his back. With his wings spread to the sides he stared into the night sky and whined:

»Ouch! Crash-landing indeed.«

Moaning in pain the raven straightened up, shook his head, and inspected his wings. After he had cleaned his feathers he looked at Finnomir, who was leaning against the tree trunk watching him.

»*Caw!* Finnomir. Beautiful night, isn't it?«

»Do you think so?«, Finnomir asked. »You hit that tree

129

pretty hard. Is that part of a beautiful night?«

The raven cocked his head and grinned and strutted to and fro in front of the butterfly. The presence of this bird made Finnomir very uncomfortable, so he called for the sleeping Wolf.

»Rogo, wake up!«

Rogo didn't move.

»Roooogoo!«, he shouted as loudly as he could. But it was of no use. The wolf slept soundly.

»Useless. *Caw!*«, the raven said impishly. »Let him sleep.«

»I don't understand.«, Finnomir said angrily. Then he sighed.

»What do you want from me now, you weird bird?«

»*Caw!* Weird bird? Weird bird?«, giggled the raven. »Visit you for the second time now, *Caw!* Told you that you must do something very important. Do you remember?«

Finnomir pretended to think hard, but that was just a game. He knew exactly what the bird had said to him on his first visit.

»You mean I should find friends for Rogo, don't you?«

The raven flapped his wings wildly and ran in circles while laughing:

»*Caw! Caw!* Friends for the wolf. Yes! Friends! Friends! Friends!«

Then he stopped and looked at Finnomir questioningly.

»Did you find a way, Finnomir?«

Finnomir looked at the sleeping wolf thoughtfully, then he shook his head in disappointment.

»No, not yet. I know Rogo has always been very lonely and I really want to help him but … «, Finnomir sighed. »I don't know how to do that.«

The raven did not answer. For a few moments he just looked at Finnomir with a grin. Then he went very close to the sleeping wolf and pecked Rogo's nose with his beak. Rogo's nose twitched a few times, but the wolf didn't appear to notice anything. Neither the ravens pecking nor the loud conversation between Finnomir and the bird could wake up the wolf. Finnomir watched it all very suspiciously.

»Why can't Rogo hear you?«

The raven grinned mischievously.

»It's not his journey. *Caw!* Not *his* journey. I thought you knew that, Finnomir.«

The raven turned his back on Finnomir and walked away

preparing to take off. He looked back over his shoulder.

»*Caw!* You have two days left before you get home, Finnomir. Come up with an idea.«

The bird spread his wings and fluttered up in the air. He flew in a circle around the tree and called:

»I will visit you again, Finnomir. One more time. *Caw!*«

And just as quickly as he had appeared, the bird flew through the treetops and vanished into the night sky.

*

Finnomir sat in the moonlight and contemplated. Why did the raven say this wasn't Rogo's journey? Rogo had travelled just as far as Finnomir. In fact, the journey was a lot more strenuous for the wolf than for Finnomir, because Finnomir had been carried by the wolf. The raven was right about one thing. Finnomir had to make sure that Rogo would no longer be lonely.

*

The next morning Rogo climbed up the mountain with Finnomir sleeping in his fur. At noon they reached the snow-covered pass. Rogo turned and looked back at the path that lay behind them. It was a cloudless day with a clear blue sky.

»Finnomir, just look! You can almost see the ocean.«

Finnomir crawled out of Rogo's fur and sat on his shoulder, but he said nothing. He looked over the world stretched out in front of his eyes; the world they had traveled through for months. He couldn't see the ocean, but he knew it was there. Remembering that he had been there created a strange feeling inside his chest. He sighed softly.

»How far is it to the clearing, Rogo?«

Rogo looked at his little companion sitting on his shoulder. Finnomir looked so tired.

»Tonight we will reach the forest on the other side of the mountain. We will spend the night there. Tomorrow you will be home again, shortly before noon, Finnomir.«

Finnomir smiled. But it was a tired smile. Then he crawled back into Rogo's fur and Rogo hurried down the mountain. He crossed the plateau where they had fought Eratogast's wolf pack. They were not attacked this time. Obviously, Mora and Pito had taken care of the two travelers' safety. Rogo followed the same little brook downhill that they had followed uphill on their outward journey. Just before the sun went down, they reached the forest.

*

Rogo placed Finnomir on a patch of moss. He picked a flower and held it out to the butterfly.

»Please drink some nectar, Finnomir.«

Rogo's voice sounded worried. The butterfly looked at the flower and blinked. Then he looked at Rogo, smiled and slowly shook his head.

»I'm not hungry, Rogo.«

Finnomir's voice was weak. He lay down on the moss and closed his eyes. Rogo covered him with a leaf, then he lay down next to the butterfly and watched over him. He was very worried. Day after day Finnomir grew weaker and he ate less. Every day a piece of his wings broke off; very little remained. Rogo sighed and closed his eyes. He was almost fallen asleep when he suddenly heard Finnomir's voice.

»Will you remember me, Rogo?«

Rogo opened his eyes in alarm. Finnomir had raised his head

and was looking at the wolf. Rogo blinked and was confused.

»What did you say, Finnomir?«

»Will you remember me?«

Rogo swallowed hard.

»Always, Finnomir«, he replied, sounding almost horrified; horrified that his companion could ask such a thing.

»Do you promise?«

»I promise, Finnomir. How could I ever forget you?«

Finnomir smiled, then he lay down and fell asleep. Rogo looked at his little friend for a while and he felt a deep pain in his chest. Then he fell asleep too.

*

Finnomir woke up because he was cold. He opened his eyes and saw that he was no longer covered. The raven stood in front of him holding the leaf in his beak. He had pulled it from Finnomir's body. He spat it out and nodded his head up and down.

»*Caw!* The sun is rising soon, Finnomir.«

»So what?«, Finnomir replied grumpily. »What do you care about the rising sun? Besides, it is still dark.«

The raven grinned at Finnomir.

»*Caw!* You will be home today. Did you do your job, Finnomir?«

Finnomir looked at the sleeping wolf. Then he looked sadly to the ground, shook his head and sobbed.

»Rogo needs friends. But I don't know how to accomplish that.«

He looked into the raven's eyes.

»I can't be here for him any longer, am I right?«

»*Caw!* You will be home soon, Finnomir.«

Finnomir wiped a tear from his cheek and sniffed.

»That does not answer my question.«

The raven strutted up and down in front of the butterfly.

»Yes it does, *caw!* Soon you will understand.«

Finnomir looked at the bird angrily.

»I don't understand anything you say. You are just annoying me. You haven't even given me your name.«

The raven stopped walking to and fro.

»My name is not important, Finnomir.«

The raven's voice had suddenly changed. He no longer cawed

and he no longer grinned. He no longer nodded his beak up and down wildly or flapped his wings uneasily. He stood in front of Finnomir with his head held up high and looked at the butterfly solemnly.

»You will come home today, Finnomir. When you are there, just follow the rainbow! Don't worry about Rogo. I know you will find a solution and I promise it will make you happy.«

The raven turned around and looked back over his shoulder at Finnomir.

»Remember the rainbow, Finnomir. Follow the rainbow!«

The raven bowed his head politely.

»I'm leaving you now. Farewell, Finnomir.«

Then he pushed himself off the ground and fluttered away. Finnomir watched the bird fly away, but soon he could no longer see because his eyes filled up with tears. Then the sun rose. A new day had started. Finnomir wiped away the tears. He took a deep breath and thought of the clearing with the big tree in the middle, and he thought of what the raven had said to him. Then he sighed.

»Today I am going home.«

It was not long before Rogo woke up and they made their way to the clearing.

*

Finnomir and Rogo reached the edge of the forest and they stood in front of the tree with the mushrooms.

»We are here, Finnomir.«

Finnomir slowly crawled out of Rogo's fur. He was weak and tired. He could hardly keep his eyes open, and the last pieces of his wings had now finally gone. Finnomir lifted his head with difficulty. He looked across the clearing and blinked. All the animals of the forest were gathered. They sat in the meadow and stared at the big tree. They had come to see the birth of the new generation of butterflies. Finnomir smiled softly because he recognized all of his friends. There they were, Mora, Aquila, Pito, Krix and Eric. The mole stood on Mora's shoulder and wept, the wild boars grunted with joy and the squirrels whisked swiftly up and down the branches of the tree. The time had come. A new generation of little butterflies slipped out of their cocoons, entered the world and stepped into their new lives. Finnomir saw the spectacle and sighed softly.

»Will you please put me in my mushroom-house,

Rogo? Right there, under this tree. It is the big mushroom with the green moss underneath.«

Rogo stared enthusiastically at the clearing and at the tree with the hatching butterflies. Then he looked at his little friend and became sad. He held out his paw and Finnomir climbed inside. The wolf placed the butterfly carefully on the soft moss under the large mushroom. Finnomir lay down and Rogo covered him with a leaf. Then he sat down next to him. Finnomir closed his eyes. He was finally home, but he was so very tired. Suddenly he had an idea and he summoned all of his strength.

»Rogo«, Finnomir whispered hoarsely.

»Yes, Finnomir?«

»Tell them about our journey.«

Rogo looked at Finnomir thoughtfully. He contemplated for a moment, then nodded.

»I will.«

»Do you promise?«

»I promise, Finnomir. I will tell them everything.«

Finnomir smiled happily. At the big tree someone shouted, »*They're pumping up their wings*«, and a murmur went through the crowd. Rogo looked mesmerized at the scenery on the clearing because he saw the birth of the butterflies for the very first time in his life.

>>Look, Finnomir! How colorful the tree has suddenly become! Isn't that wonderful?<<

Finnomir was happy. He was pleased with Rogo's enthusiasm, and he knew for certain that Rogo would never be lonely again. Then he closed his eyes.

>>Look, Finnomir! They are flapping their wings. They are about to fly.<<

Finnomir did not answer and the wolf looked down at his little friend.

>>Finnomir, do you hear? They are flying. Finnomir?...Finnomir!<<

In Finnomir's ears the sound of Rogo's voice was waning. Then the world turned dark and silent.

The Sun

Finnomir found himself standing all alone in the clearing in front of the big tree. He saw the shadow of his body on the ground in front of him and this shadow was unusually large. He looked back over his shoulders and when he saw his mighty wings he started laughing happily. *»I will fly!«*, he thought and spread out his magnificent wings, and the purple and blue colors shone brightly through the green grass. Effortlessly he flapped his wings and rose up into the air, and a rainbow of bright and glittering colors appeared before him stretching out from the ground high up to the blue sky, and the sun's rays sparkled all around it. Finnomir remembered: *When you are there, follow the rainbow*, the raven had said. Finnomir did just that. He flew along the band of bright colors and ascended higher and higher towards the blue sky.

He looked down and saw the world underneath grow smaller. Then he looked up and saw the sun waiting for him at the end of the rainbow. She smiled and waved to him. He flew to her and the sun greeted him and said:

»Turn around and look, Finnomir! This is the world.«

Finnomir saw the world below and he was amazed. He saw the

forest; and all his friends were sitting in the clearing. Rogo was with them too, and Rogo was happy. Then Finnomir looked across the forest and saw the mountains. Snow covered the peaks and the fog passed through the valleys. He looked further and he saw the ocean in the far distance. The ocean was blue and green and dolphins were jumping over high waves.

»The world is beautiful!«, said Finnomir, and he asked the sun:

»I was down there once and now I am here?«

»Yes«, said the sun. »And now you will stay here.«

Finnomir looked down at the world with joy while the sun spoke to him:

»Look at your life, Finnomir! You made a lot of friends.«

A big smile formed on Finnomir's face.

»Yes. The best friends one could ask for.«

And the sun continued:

»You fought against wolves in the mountains. No butterfly has ever done that.«

Finnomir's eyes widened.

»Yes, that was exciting.«

142

The sun pointed to the mountains.

»You were on the highest peak, higher than any butterfly before. You danced in the snow and saw my sunset from up there on the distant horizon.«

»Yes. It was beautiful to be up there.«

»You travelled through the wilderness to the ocean and you swam on a dolphin.«

Finnomir laughed.

»Yes. Didu is a funny guy.«

»You gave the wolf a reason to live. He was your most loyal companion and he risked his life for you. Because of you he now has a lot of friends. He will never be lonely again.«

Finnomir bowed his head thoughtfully and he nodded and smiled contently.

»Yes that is true. It makes me happy to know that Rogo has friends now.«

Then the sun spoke in a soft voice.

»Look at me, Finnomir!«

And Finnomir looked at the sun.

»You were sad because you had no wings. You were so sad, you wanted to end your life. Now think about it! Your

143

life was a great adventure. If you had had wings, you wouldn't have gone on this journey, you wouldn't have had all these adventures and Rogo would still be a lonely and angry beast, lurking in the dark forest.«

Finnomir's eyes widened in astonishment. Then he laughed out loud with joy:

»I understand now! My life had a purpose! My life was good. It was the best life that I could have and I would not trade it for anything.«

The sun smiled contentedly. She took Finnomir by his hands and they laughed and danced together on top of the rainbow.

The clearing

Rogo stepped out of the darkness of the forest into the sunlight of the clearing. One of the groundhogs saw him first. It whistled loudly and called:

»Watch out! A wolf!«

Terrified the animals turned around instantly and stared at the grey menacing animal, but Mora raised a hand and calmed them.

»Don't be afraid, my friends. This is Rogo, Finnomir's companion.«

The animals breathed a sigh of relief. Then they put their heads together and muttered. Mora smiled at Rogo.

»We've been waiting for you, Rogo. Say, where's Finnomir?«

Rogo looked back to the edge of the forest and the tree with the mushrooms. He sighed briefly and thought: *I can still feel him sitting on my shoulder*. Then he looked at Mora and, in her eyes, he saw that she hoped for good news. Rogo's heart grew heavy and he looked down at the ground. He didn't know what to say to Mora. He contemplated desperately, but then he remembered Finnomir's last words and he regained courage and began to smile. He raised his head, looked at the assembled community, and said with a loud and confident voice:

»Animals of the forest, please listen to me! I want to tell you a story.«

The animals stared curiously at Rogo, but they kept muttering. The eagle spread one of his wings and everyone instantly fell silent. He kindly nodded to the wolf.

»Speak, Rogo.«

Rogo nodded back gratefully. He sat down in the grass in front of the animals and they looked at him with curiosity and excitement. The wolf looked back at the edge of the forest one last time, then he took a deep breath and began to tell:

»On a big blue ball circling the sun. On a continent unknown and unsung. In a forest that has no name. There grows a tree in the middle of a clearing. And amidst the twigs and leaves and acorns, Finnomir the butterfly was born. ... «

The End

Printed in Great Britain
by Amazon